Scalpel And Hatchet

By

John G. McConahy

authorHOUSE

1663 Liberty Drive, Suite 200
Bloomington, Indiana 47403
(800) 839-8640
www.authorhouse.com

© 2004 John G. McConahy.
All Rights Reserved.

No part of this book may be reproduced, stored in a retrieval system, or transmitted by any means without the written permission of the author.

First published by AuthorHouse 07/27/04

ISBN: 1-4184-6916-5 (sc)
ISBN: 1-4184-6915-7 (dj)

Printed in the United States of America
Bloomington, Indiana

This book is printed on acid-free paper.

Acknowledgement

This manuscript would still be a shambles had it not been rescued from the computer by my daughter Elizabeth Randall Gerbino. Randall read and reread the book, correcting spelling, syntax, sequence, and a million other things that can occur. I am most grateful.

Likewise, I must thank Betty Holmes McConahy, my wife, who also read and reread the book and allowed me to go blissfully on my way. I love those two girls for their help and forbearance.

Finally, my thanks to John N. Gerbino for his design and artwork on the cover of the book.

Jack McConahy Hobe Sound, Florida
Scalpel and Hatchet

Prologue

The early days of the American Colonies were difficult in many ways. Not the least of the difficulties that faced the settlers was the constant threat of the French and their savage Indian allies, the Algonquin. Those early settlers lived always in fear of the terrors of Indian war. There were many who learned the loneliness of dying in the flames of a burning frontier. It is doubtful, indeed, if the colonies could have survived were it not for the Long House; the massive brooding, menacing, yet protective blanket that was flung over the northern portion of the English colonies from the banks of the Hudson to the shores of Lake Erie. This protective blanket, the Long House, was the confederation of the Seneca, Cayuga, Onondaga, Oneida, and Mohawk Indian Nations. They called themselves the Hodenosaunee, translated as "The people who are better than other people." Other Indian tribes called them Agonuschioni or Irakwai. The English knew them as the Five Nations, but the French name Iroquois remains as the common name for them down through the years.

Only a student of Colonial days and earlier years would be aware that this Confederation, the Hodenosaunee, in the mid-seventeenth century, drove the French and their Algonquin allies across eastern Canada and then laid siege to Montreal. In the ultimate peace settlement the Hodenosaunee agreed, grudgingly, that they would not interfere in the struggle for supremacy between the English and French. In return, the French indicated they would not trespass on nor cross over the lands of the Five Nations. Although there were minor sneaky transgressions, the large war parties of the Algonquin and French were forced to travel east of the Hudson or west of Lake Erie in their raids on the Colonies. The vast wilderness of Penn's woods was apparently wide open to colonization. Much of this wilderness, however, was the hunting grounds of the Hodenosaunee. Would-be trespassers of any color, for the most part, dared not to enter without the permission of the Hodenosaunee. Throughout the history of the Five Nations there were many prophecies. The prophecy told here is the story of "The Hatchet"!

Chapter I

The fall sun burned fiercely on the leaves of autumn and reflected the glory of their colors in the smoothly running waters of Minquas Kill. That Saturday, August 18, 1684, was merely a fleck of dust in the path of mankind, but it was to be significant later because of the squalling baby boy that was born on that day. Axel Bjorgenson, one of the original settlers of Minguas Kill, had a beautiful daughter, Karen, who had but one flaw. In a day when the average man stood a mere five foot four inches tall, Karen stood six feet two in her bare feet. As one might imagine, it was love at first sight for the lass when Karen looked up at the towering six foot six inches of the handsome Captain General of William Penn's militia, Captain Thomas MacKaye. The good Captain, in turn, was overwhelmed by the beautiful woman who could, in fact, stand nearly eye-to-eye with him. Ere long they married. The fruit of that marriage was produced on that August eighteenth in the raw light of the afternoon. That babe, a son, was large at birth and the touch of redness in his black shock of hair gave a hint of the fury and danger that could, and would, come from the man to be.

"Who could be so fortunate?" cried a happy Captain MacKaye. "Here am I in the company of most of my good and close friends. I have a loving and beautiful wife. Presently she is at home nursing my, or rather our, newborn son whom we shall probably name Thomas Todd Mackaye, after me. Now I have here in my hand, my orders to go forth, together with my family, to the Carolinas where I am to represent my leader and good friend, William Penn. He does indeed do me great honor." Pausing for a moment, Captain MacKaye gazed reflectively into the fire. The tavern was still and even the great logs of the fireplace seemed to crackle more softly than usual. The listeners were attentively silent. Dropping his voice, the Captain spoke quietly. "My heart is filled with sadness for I must leave you, my good friends, as well as this beloved place I shall always call my home. It has come to me", continued the Captain, "that my duty calls me away from much that I hold dear, but I must go, and I do want you to know that there is much joy for me as I look to the future. I welcome this new adventure!"

The Captain looked from face to face, nodding to each in turn and finally, raising his hand, he continued. "Drink up my friends. Should the good Lord will that I cannot be amongst you again, look you for my son to return here to the place of his birth. You can be sure that at the very least, one of us will come back. This place is, in truth, our home! Prophecy, such as this of mine, will not be lightly forgotten." They were brave words and stoutly spoken.

Captain MacKaye continued after a thirst-quenching drink from his glass, "On the morrow our ship, the Bonny Lass, sails for Carolina." Sweeping his hand in the direction of a distinguished looking, bearded gentleman sitting on his right. He said, "With us, returning to his home in Carolina, sails my new found friend, Doctor Henry Woodward. Though our acquaintance has been short, Doctor Woodward, good man that he is, has consented to stand as godfather for my son when we arrive in the Carolinas."

Pausing for a short breath, he added, "In truth, as of today, Doctor Woodward is my only acquaintance in the Carolinas. Should anything happen to this babe's parents, Karen and myself, who else would be there to look after the boy?"

Raising his cup the Captain cried out, "Stand, my friends, and drink a cup to this good man." Forthwith, the tavern rang with "Huzzah" and "Good Cheer"!

Turning, he pointed toward a bulky figure that was standing back in the shadowed corner of the Ordinary, where the greatcoats were hanging.

"Gentlemen", he said, "It is the custom of our family for a newborn lad to have two godfathers and a godmother. The godmother for the babe we will have to name in Carolina. However, I happen to know a man here who is well equipped to teach the youngster the ways of this wild country."

"Gentlemen", he continued, as he nodded toward the burly, buckskin clad, Susquehannock Indian standing in that corner, "I would ask you to drink to my choice for the other godfather. Heathen he might be, but he is my friend and faithful servant. He has agreed to accompany us on our voyage, to live with us in Carolina, and to watch over the boy."

If you will then," he said, raising his cup, "a nog to Atsego."

Gravely the mugs were raised again in the direction of the patient Indian, and the flash of the firelight was reflected on the teeth of that grim figure. A new arrival, fresh from England, would have considered the choice of the Indian, Atsego, to be the godparent of a baby boy to be quite strange. However these men who lived in the New World, understood and nodded their heads in approval of this selection, as they raised their mugs to their lips.

Chapter II

The sun was barely peeking over the eastern horizon when the tide turned and the Bonny Lass cast off her ties and, freed of restraint, turned her bow down the river. Under half sail she eagerly headed for the sea.

Doctor Woodward, old sea dog that he once was, thrilled once again to the plunge of the ship's deck as she plowed into the surge of the Atlantic. At times, Atsego and the Captain would walk around the deck, but most of the time they spent below with Karen and the baby.

Though the skies throughout the day were alternately cloudy and sunny and the water was calm, Woodward had an uneasy feeling in his bones. Finally, he made his way to the bridge. He had noted that all day the captain of the Bonny Lass had not strayed too far from the deck and the helmsman.

When Woodward voiced his unease to the man, that worthy fellow smiled and said, "You've been here before, I know. I've had the feeling for the past two days and now, if you look, you'll find that the barometer is falling rapidly." With a sigh he looked out over the sea. Finally he turned back, saying with a wave of his arm, "It looks so placid and safe but, like you, I fear we're in for a blow in a matter of hours."

Woodward nodded in agreement and noted that some of the crew was busily battening the hatches while others were lashing down every loose object on deck. The deck cannons had already been secured. The ship was proceeding under half sail as darkness began to gather around them and the wind began to rise.

Chapter III

"Cape Hatteras hath a blow in store for those who pass her howling door!"

The groaning timbers of the Bonny Lass told the story of her torture! The gale was beating furiously on her port side, striving to drive the battered ship toward the storm-lashed shores, as she painfully beat her way southward. While the wind whipped the rigging, the wild waves shook the ship as a dog playfully shakes a stick.

As the storm raged, below deck Atsego sat on the floor of their tiny cabin braced in a corner with the tiny babe in his huge arms. Meanwhile, trying to stand, holding onto anything solid against the convulsive pitching of the ship, Captain MacKaye and Dr. Woodward hovered over the unmoving figure of Karen, lying so terribly quiet and still in the bunk.

At dawn the day had been bright and sunny but, as the morning wore on, sullen blue-black clouds blotted out the sun and its warm, friendly light. A gray, hostile stillness replaced the sun. The first severe blast of the gale force wind from the storm had suddenly heeled the Bonny Lass hard upon her side and all aboard were flung about in savage fashion. Karen unfortunately was standing at that moment and was thrown across the tiny cabin. Her head struck with a smashing impact on the hard corner of the built-in bunk. She collapsed without a word upon the floor and never moved again

Doctor Woodward was immediately at the side of the stricken woman. Gently his fingers probed the bloody bruised area of impact behind Karen's right ear. Palpating the area of damage, his sensitive fingers could feel the crepitation of bone fragment beneath his fingertips.

Gravely the Doctor shook his head. Looking up at the stunned, white-faced captain, he said, "Tom, my friend, I do not know how to tell you this. The blow to her head when she was thrown has shattered the bones of her skull. Her coma, you can see, is rapidly deepening. Her pulse is so thin it is almost non-existent, and the pitching of the ship is aggravating the situation. At the moment, under these circumstances, there is absolutely nothing I can do. Karen is in the hands of God, and, I fear, she will be with him in a very few minutes. I am so terribly sorry, my friend."

With a heart-rending sob, Captain MacKaye sat on the bunk beside his motionless wife and buried his face in his hands. Softly he cried out, "Karen, oh my Karen." Almost as if she had heard him, and perhaps she did, Karen opened her eyes, sighed briefly and died as gently as she had lived.

With a bitter cry of disbelief, the Captain leaped to his feet and staggered down the companionway; so overwrought with grief that he hardly noticed the heaving deck beneath his feet. Blindly he climbed the ladder, and on reaching the sodden, storm lashed deck outside, he reeled over to the pitching rail. There he stood alone in his agony while his friends, carrying his now motherless son, started to climb the ladder after him.

It was then that the ship with a scream of tortured timbers, accompanied by a horrifying crash, struck a hidden reef in the roaring surf. In a trice, the main mast gave way at its base with a splintering noise and plunged into the maelstrom. When the crash occurred a mighty comber swept the full length of the ship. Captain MacKaye, standing at the rail, disappeared under the massive wave and was seen no more. He was thus reunited with his beloved Karen.

Below deck Doctor Woodward was hurled from the ladder and flew head over heels down the companionway. Atsego hung onto the ladder for a moment but was finally torn loose and thrown across the way to crash into the bulkhead. Fortunately, he was able to shield the babe from smashing against the wall by twisting his body so that his shoulder took the force of the impact.

Clambering to his feet against the steep pitch of the flooring that heaved like a crazed thing from side to side, up and down, and as it seemed, around and around, Atsego made his way, holding the babe in his left arm, down the narrow aisle. There the Doctor was slowly raising himself to his hands and knees. With his free arm,

Atsego grasped the Doctor's shirt with his huge fist and lifted him to his feet.

"Must get out," grunted the Indian, and by brute strength he carried the slight doctor and the tiny, squalling baby through knee-deep water back to the stair ladder. The stair that normally would rise with a slight angle off the vertical, now lay almost flat. It rose and fell with the hammering surge of the relentless waves as they beat against the reef. With a firm grasp of his right arm around the Doctor's waist, and the baby firmly in the clutch of his left, Atsego struggled along the ladder and out through the hatch. Once outside and clear of the hatch, Atsego took a deep breath and dove with his helpless burdens into the foaming, churning waters.

They had barely gotten the first taste of brine in their mouths when the next breaker caught them in its salty arms and carried them on its crest a full hundred yards from the stricken vessel. Holding tightly to his precious cargo, Atsego ascended to the surface with powerful thrusts of his legs. There they all had an opportunity for a brief gasp of mist filled air.

Behind them with an apparent last roar of defiance, the Bonny Lass seemed to explode under the inexorable drive of the waves. For an instant the ship was lying there against the reef in its agony and, in the next moment, it shattered and literally blew to pieces. Masts and timbers flew into the air and were whisked away into nothingness by the screaming force of the gale winds. Cordage lashed the air like giant whips. With a mighty splash, a huge section of the mizzenmast plunged into the water close by the struggling trio.

Doctor Woodward was able to reach out and seize hold on a rope trailing away from the mast section. Still held in the firm grasp of Atsego, Woodward managed to pull the little group over to the mast. Now the doctor took the baby in one arm, holding onto the mast with the other. Atsego, hands now free, was then able to lash them all to the spar. In that fashion they were able to keep their heads above the water, clinging together for warmth throughout the night.

After a seeming eternity, the slashing impact of the salty spray and the fierce beating of the waves began to subside as the gale blew out. Morning dawned to find the broken mast with its exhausted passengers being slowly driven onto a barren, sandy, yet gratefully found, shore. Of the Bonny Lass, or any of her passengers or crew, including the father of the baby, naught was to be seen. The raucous cry of a seagull was the only sight or sound.

Staggering with weariness onto that desolate sandy shore, the powerful arms of Atsego both held the baby and kept a reeling Woodward from falling on the sand.

With a voice raw from the salt, Atsego said, "Just a little bit more, good Doctor. We must get ourselves and this brave warrior into the woodland before the sun shines strong."

Atsego then carried the limp but still living baby in one arm and helped the Doctor to stagger across the beach to the leafy green of the forest edge some hundred yards away. Once under the protective cover of the trees, Atsego placed the baby on the ground beside the exhausted Woodward and grunted, "Doctor, watch over this tiny warrior until I return. He must be fed, and soon." With those words Atsego turned and slipped into the forest. The baby slept and, finally, the doctor's head dropped back and the two of them lay quietly side-by-side.

The doctor awoke with a guilty start when Atsego tapped him on the shoulder. Quickly glancing over at the baby beside him and reassured by the steady breathing of that weary, little chest, Woodward turned his attention to Atsego, and with some trepidation, saw five strange Indians standing behind him. Atsego face broke into a smile. "Tuscaroras", he said, "Totem brothers." Then, and only then, when even his mighty strength was exhausted, did Atsego sit down on the ground beside the Doctor and the baby.

Chapter IV

The glaring sun baked the ground. A rare puff of wind would occasionally create a tiny, miniature tornado-like, dust devil that would collapse feebly back to earth almost as quickly as it formed. Henry Woodward, physician and surgeon, now sopping with perspiration, cursed softly under his breath as he strode along the street. He was facing a problem that made his past seem insignificant. And what a past! He smiled as he thought of his carefree days with the Tuscaroras with whom he had been a hostage for a short time. And then he had had some bad times when he was captured and imprisoned by the Spaniards in Saint Augustine until Searle and his buccaneers came along and rescued him.

"I did get back to Carolina," mused the doctor, "after half a lifetime of wild action, but now, after years of sedentary peace, I am verging on an even greater adventure that truly terrifies me. Nevertheless, it must be done."

Breaking stride, Dr. Woodward placed his bag on the dusty street and turned back to the odd pair behind him. Patiently standing there was the huge, swarthy Indian Atsego, and peering contentedly from the Indian's arms was a tiny white baby boy. The contrast made the doctor smile.

"My friend", said Doctor Woodward to the Indian, Atsego, " it seems that you and I are no longer just godparents to this boy but, in reality, his only parents. There's no one else to accept this responsibility. I would like you to come, if you will, to live with me and we will raise this youngster. It's bound to be a difficult task in a womanless house, but I will teach him his letters and later introduce him to the field of medicine. You can teach him the lore of the wilderness. Will you do it?"

Atsego looked Woodward full in the face. Then the faint trace of a smile crossed his usually impassive countenance. Atsego nodded his acceptance of this new responsibility.

Woodward smiled in turn and said, "Good! As you know the lad's dying mother had no breath for a name, nor for that matter, did his father. I guess that it is only fitting that we name him for his father. We shall christen him as Thomas Todd MacKaye."

The black eyes of the Susquehannock gleamed, and he nodded his agreement.

Chapter V

Spanish moss hung from the trees like bearded elders in a council center.

A gentle breeze caused the moss to sway soundlessly in the trees that circled the little forest glade. A swamp deer, nibbling at a grassy copse within the glade, stirred nervously at a slight rustling of the leaves. The low brush on the down-wind side of the clearing was gently and silently parted. There was a whirring "thwang", and then a "thud", as an arrow struck home in the side of the deer just behind the shoulder. For a moment the deer stood there as a quivering shudder ran over his body, and then he went to his knees. The crackling of the brush made by the rangy, broad shouldered man who burst into the clearing made the deer rise to his feet and prepare to run.

As the deer took his first tentative step, the right arm of the man, hatchet in hand, swung forward. The tomahawk came spinning, end over end, across the open space and struck the deer in the throat, knocking him back to the ground. In a trice, the man was on the animal, but even as he drove his knife into the heart, his thoughts were on the whistling, gasping of air from the slash in the throat made by the tomahawk.

"I wonder," he thought, "if one could live and breathe through a hole in the windpipe? There certainly is very little bleeding from this gash."

Then he turned his thoughts back to the moment and muttered to himself, "Atsego would be very critical of my throw after all he has taught me. As often as I have practiced, I must admit it was not a good throw. Nevertheless, none of the Tuscaroras, or even Atsego, can throw the hatchet as well as I."

Now he began to work. Laying the deer on its side on the slope of a little hill with the head on the uphill side, he made a small slit in the belly skin. He then inserted two fingers in the slit, holding the knife blade between the fingers, edge out, and finished his cut to, and around the genitals and anal orifice. It was only a matter of a few minutes before he had the deer dressed out. From the neat pile of internal organs lying alongside the deer he removed the heart and liver. Tom placed those organs in a large leather pouch that he attached to his belt.

"Neatly done", he thought, "and well it should be. My father Atsego trained me well in the ways of the wilderness, and this is but a part of it."

Shrugging, he lifted the deer and threw it easily over his shoulder. Silently he slipped through the forest until he came to a well-beaten trail. Once there, he broke into the steady, ground-covering lope that was also a part of Atsego's training.

As he ran, his mind turned toward his other father, the Doctor. "He too trained me well in my letters and as his medical apprentice, I too am called Doctor. Many are the hours I have spent at his side. I wonder what he meant this morning when he said 'I must learn some of the niceties of life?' After three years as his apprentice, he says I am as skilled as any doctor in the Carolinas."

A half hour of Tom's easy gait brought the first houses of Charles Town into view. Turning away from the dirt street that ran through the middle of the village, the young man trotted along a path that followed the outlying fields. That path finally brought him to the garden gate that led to a white-framed house. This house served the dual purpose of the surgery for both doctors and also as home for them all. In the shadow of the gate stood the Susquehannock, Atsego.

As tall and broad shouldered as the Indian was, the young white man matched him height for height and shoulder for shoulder. Though his mature figure was heavier, even Atsego acknowledged the raw, unleashed power of the younger man.

"Well done warrior," said Atsego, "Give me the deer I will play the squaw who will dress the meat. You, Tawde, must hurry and cleanse yourself. The Doctor awaits you in his surgery."

Stepping quickly over to the pump, and slipping out of his leather breeches, Tom washed under the cool water. Atsego laid the deer aside and pumped the water while the young man bathed. A belt of white skin around the loins of the youth stood out in sharp contrast to the tan on the rest of his body and seemed to flash in the shadows of the two huge figures.

After drying himself on a length of dry bleached muslin that Atsego had thoughtfully provided, the young man turned toward the house. A short run and a leap carried him to the slanting roof of the woodshed attached to the back of the house. He trotted up the slope of the roof, and gracefully dove through the open window of his room. Behind, Atsego chuckled as he lifted the carcass of the deer from the ground.

Chapter VI

"The sweet taste of your urine", said Doctor Woodward, "would seem to clinch the diagnosis in your case, Mister Randall, when one couples it with your lassitude, thirst, and the frequent and copious urination that has been troubling you. You must eat less of honey and syrup with corn cakes. It is well for you to eat meat, but you certainly must cut in half that which you eat, if you wish to live a long and untroubled life. And you should strive to lose at least a stone of weight."

With a sigh, as Mister Randall closed the door behind him and left, the Doctor wearily raised himself from the chair at his desk. Heavily he walked across to where his assistant was hovering over a patient.

"Very nice, Doctor MacKaye," he said as he glanced over the shoulder of his young protégé. He surveyed with satisfaction the neat incision the younger man had made in the leg of the elderly Mister Landrum.

"Very nice, indeed. That is very laudable pus. The boil should heal without event." After a moments pause, he added, "Thomas when you have finished here, I would have you come into the library. I believe that the time has come for us to make some plans for your future." Gravely nodding his head, Woodward turned and slowly left the room.

Curious as to the meaning of the Doctor's words, Tom quickly cleansed the wound and applied a poultice. Following the limping departure of the grateful Mister Landrum, Tom hurriedly washed his hands and hastily went to the library. There he found Atsego, as well as Doctor Woodward, awaiting him. Atsego was sitting quietly on a floor pillow, propped against the wall. Henry Woodward, dignified and thin, stood before the fireplace. His head was bowed as if in thought, his hand resting lightly on the mantle.

As Tom passed through the library door, Doctor Woodward looked up and gave him a fond smile. "Sit you down Thomas", he said, "Sit you there in my chair, across from Atsego, where we can both see you well. No, no. Sit there, for I must stand and walk as I talk."

Sighing deeply, the good Doctor continued. "It is, suddenly, as if eighteen years were only yesterday, and you were still a babe. Now, as I look at the size of you here, I am forced to acknowledge that our yesterdays have flown! Yes," he mused sadly, "It has come. Today is here, and now we must plan for your future, if we can, and the good Lord wills it to be so."

"Thomas", he said in a firm voice, "When the good Lord took your true parents to Himself, Atsego and I, as your designated godparents, saw fit to undertake your education in such a broad manner that you might well be able to adjust to, or cope with, almost any situation that you could possibly encounter in this wild land of ours. Up to a certain point, we two, who have been your teachers from infancy, have been uniquely qualified to do exactly that. We believe that we have been very successful. Atsego's success is because he is a magnificent, intelligent product of the wilderness that lies in the shadow, only a step beyond the light of our lamps. My success lies in the fact that I am a man of profession, as well as a man with a broad background in letters and culture."

"Atsego has told me, admiringly I might add, that you are the equal in stealth and in your ability to survive in the wild of any Indian in the forest. He says further, that physically you are as strong as any man he has ever known, that you are his peer in every weapon, and that your skill in throwing the tomahawk surpasses that of anyone he has ever seen. Atsego took you with him on several occasions to live with the Tuscarora. You were formally adopted by the Turtle Clan of the Tuscarora, and I am aware that you are fluent in their language. That is important because it is also the language of the Cherokee and the Five Nations. All this being true, and I am sure that it is, you are indeed a formidable savage. Atsego and I both agree that this phase of your education is completed. We believe that it is well to leave this present phase behind you at the present time. The attempts of certain white colonists to take over the lands of the Tuscarora and to enslave them for work in the fields can only result in a war that the Indians cannot win. We hope to spare you that."

"In regard to your education in the civilized world, I can tell you that there are not ten men in Carolina that are better lettered than are you. Indeed, in the process of teaching you, I have learned much myself. Here with us in this small provincial town you have lived a rather sequestered life! You may not, as yet, be aware that the so-called civilized world can at times be a dangerous place. I have known this. Over the years some of my friends from my checkered past have visited with us to educate you in another fashion. With the help of these friends we have been able to develop your martial skills. With your natural ability you have become a fine swordsman and an excellent pistol shot. I hope you will have no need for these talents, but you may."

"Professionally, Thomas", the Doctor continued, "except for the knowledge and awareness that only the experience of passing years can teach you, you are as well trained as any physician in the Colonies, and better by far than most."

Pausing for a moment to marshal his thoughts, Doctor Woodward continued to speak. "Atsego and I are proud of our protégé, but there is another aspect of life that we, of necessity, have neglected. This phase of which I speak lies beyond the reach of Atsego, and it is now impossible for me to see you through it. In truth, I must point out to you that Carolina, after all, is only a provincial colony. There is much to be learned in England that does not exist here."

"Experience, Doctor Thomas", said Woodward with a wry smile, "is a great teacher. Lacking long experience with the approach of death or perhaps from being too close to me, you have not, Tom, been aware of my physical disintegration over the past year. Nay, sit still my beloved Tom. Atsego has known for several months and I for ten or more of this tumor in my abdomen. That it is malignant, I am sure. I know that my time is limited to a very few months. I am leaving everything to you and Atsego. He will continue to live here."

Tom sat in stunned silence looking at the gentle Doctor at whose feet he had spent so many childhood evenings. At those feet he had learned his letters. His words choked in his throat. His blurred vision saw the truth in the look of pain that had crossed the face of the usually impassive Atsego.

Finally Tom bowed his head and, as the tears streamed down his face, said in a broken voice, "No, I did not know."

"Tom," said the Doctor quietly, "I have lived a very full life. I have, as you know, sailed with privateers, lived with the Indians, been imprisoned by the Spaniards, and been rescued by, of all people, pirates. I have practiced as a physician, a work that I love. Best of all, for the past eighteen years God has blessed me with a son whom I have lived to see become a man. I feel that my work is complete. I am tired. I have lived beyond that span of years that God allotted to man. Death and I are old acquaintances. I do not fear him."

"Now, Tom, let me continue and explain what Atsego and I have been unable to teach you. You have been raised in a womanless house and you need to know their gentle ways and wisdom. Most of them have steel, unrecognized by many, in their spirit, that many men lack. The facet of your education that has been, not neglected, but rather postponed, is knowledge of the culture of the old world. I have little doubt that, in the end, you will choose to live here in the Americas. However, I feel you should know first hand the customs and way of life of England. Atsego and I wish to complete and refine the training we swore in the name of your true parents that we would provide for you eighteen years ago when we carried you out of the raging sea onto that sandy Hatteras beach."

"I have arranged your passage for the morrow on the brig Warwick Castle which sails on the morning tide for Plymouth. At Plymouth you will take the stage for London. Once in London you are to make inquiry for Leicester Square, and the offices of my old friend, Doctor Stephen Beckwith. Years ago I made these plans with Doctor Beckwith and his reply to my last letter arrived five days ago on that same Warwick Castle. Doctor Beckwith has agreed to accept you as an associate for a year. Furthermore, he has promised that you will be exposed to those cultural portions of English life that are not to be found in the Colonies. You will be privileged to reside with Doctor Beckwith and his most gracious wife, the Lady Mary. Moreover, Lady Mary has promised that you will be exposed to the feminine side of life that, I fear, has been sadly lacking for you here in this household."

Walking over to the sideboard where three glasses of Port were already poured, the white haired Doctor spoke briskly, "It is probably best that we have been forced to take action in such haste to avoid a long and traumatic farewell. It is likely that after tomorrow we shall not meet again. I want you to remember that only through the memory of men does the life of a man on this earth live on."

"Your belongings, Tom, are already packed. Your purse is already in the pocket of your sailing suit. Since the preparations are all in readiness, let we three then have this evening and our memories together. Come lad! Come Atsego! Let us drink and look forward to new adventures with heartiness, friendship, and a dry eye!"

Chapter VII

The summons to the Court came as a complete surprise to Howard, Lord Faversham, who had always considered himself a somewhat rural lord. When he knelt before the King, he bowed his head and then raised his face to that of the Monarch in expectation of a reason for his summons to the Court. Two days earlier Faversham and his wife had been busily entertaining Lydia Batesford, Lady Mary's sister, who was visiting them from the Colonies. Out of the proverbial "blue sky", a rather peremptory order was delivered to Faversham by a royal messenger on a well-lathered horse.

"The King is desirous of the immediate presence of Lord Faversham." Now here he was at Court and the King was speaking.

"We are informed, Faversham, that you have some acquaintance with the Crown Colonies in the Americas, and that you have a desire to see them at first hand. We have also been apprised that you are a man of intelligence, good judgment, and fairness. Further, we are told of your absolute allegiance to the Crown. Is this not true?"

Faversham was stunned and, for the moment, voiceless. He had no great objection to a visit to the Colonies, but then again, he had never had a burning desire to see them. Someone had evidently recommended him to the King for this assignment but, for the life of him, he could not imagine who or why. Nonetheless, whatever he thought, he knew the answer to the King's question must be "Yes" or the King might infer a lack of allegiance that could sometimes be fatal. Therefore, since it would appear that he had no alternative, he bowed before the Monarch, smiled broadly and mumbled weakly, "This is so, Sire".

Pleased, the King looked down on the kneeling Lord and said, "We need the presence of a firm, yet fair, hand in the Carolinas. We are told that the savages there have started a war against our settlers and that the war may have something to do with some enslavement of those savages. Therefore, it pleases us to appoint you as Governor General of the Carolinas, and we do order you to settle this matter in a satisfactory manner. We would have you depart for the Colonies some two months hence. Sooner, if possible."

Faversham could only accept his mission with a weak smile in an attempt to appear pleased. He left the presence of the King and walked in a dazed fashion past the soldiers guarding the great hall and blindly down the street. The open doors of a church seemed to beckon to him and so he walked up the steps and entered the cool and comforting shadows within. After a period of reflection when his jangled nerves had settled, he was able to accept that, like it or not, he had no choice. He was going to the New World. After accepting that realization, he was able to rise and return to the street.

Emerging from the church, Faversham realized that the narrow walkway on the other side of the street led to the back of the tavern where he was lodging. After waiting to allow a coach and four to pass, he crossed and went up the walkway. He entered at the back entry to the tavern and went quietly up the back staircase to his room. When Faversham began to open the door to his room, he became aware of the conversation beneath the balcony on which he stood. Paying no attention to the conversation, he began to enter his room, pondering as he did how he would break the news to his wife and what could they do with their daughter, Nancy. Then the men who were talking mentioned his name. Curious, he went to the rail of the balcony and listened.

"My Lord, it was clever indeed for you to suggest Faversham for the post in the Colonies. He, no doubt, is wondering how he could have been chosen for the post. Now you are clear to suggest to the King that it would be a kindness to Faversham if the King would invite the daughter to be a Lady in Waiting at Court. There you will have the time and the opportunity to seduce her!" With those words, the conversation began to trail away as the speakers went out the tavern door.

Leaning over the rail, Faversham caught a glimpse of the pair as they stepped out onto the street. One of the men he recognized vaguely as one of the King's Ministers, a man who bore a well-deserved reputation as a rake. The other man was a red-coated Major, a bully swordsman named Drummond.

Drummond's last words, as the two stepped out onto the street, hung like a cloud over Faversham's head.

"Were it not for your clever plan to get Faversham out of the way, I might have had to oblige you by challenging him to a duel. As a matter of fact, I may still do that if the opportunity presents itself."

Faversham's news of the King's decision at first caused stunned consternation in his household. Then Lydia Batesford began to tell them about the unbounded opportunities that existed in the New World, and they all began to talk rationally of the possibilities. Lydia, in turn, was hopeful that his Lordship might feel that her husband, Major Batesford, could be useful in a military post, possibly in the Carolinas..

"I declare, I would fain get him away from the tavern life in Philadelphia", she said. "He is rather a dear, but beastly when he drinks!"

Satisfied that his wife was now enthusiastic, Faversham turned to his newly found problem, his daughter. To his utter amazement, she was excited and anxious to go and see the Colonies. The Lord had already told his wife in privacy of the conversation he had overheard. She turned now to her sister and said, "Lydia, you are already leaving in five days. We have a world of packing to do. If it were possible for Nancy to get ready on such short notice, perhaps she could go on ahead to Philadelphia with you. Later, when we have arrived in Carolina, she could join us there.

"Oh, I can be ready, I can be ready! Would you please take me with you Aunt Lydia?"

Smiling at the girl's enthusiasm, Aunt Lydia put her arm around her niece's shoulders and answered, "I should certainly love to have your company during that long and boring trip, and it would be a pleasure for me to have you in Philadelphia!"

An unseen, but almost audible sound of relief emanated from the interlocked eyes of the girl's parents.

Chapter VIII

The candelabra, hanging from the ceiling of the great hall, and the sconces on the wall that reflected the gleam of their candles in the mirrors behind them, seemed to move in a flowing movement, as the couples swayed and bent in a graceful minuet on the floor below. The host, Arthur, Lord Pomeroy, one gouty foot raised and resting upon a pillowed stool, was sitting at the far end of the hall. Pomeroy's somewhat bored visage brightened visibly when his eye fell on the graceful couple who had just moved in front of him in the dance. It was always a pleasure to watch his slender wife with her partner, the towering Doctor, as they moved through the intricate steps of the dance. "Would," thought Pomeroy, "that the Doctor could cure my gout as cleverly as he removed the thorn from my foot!"

On the floor, an amused smile played for a moment across Tom's face as he bowed from the waist to his dance partner, Lady Jane Pomeroy. The swarthy tan of the Doctor's face stood out in sharp contrast to his hair, powdered white to the ultra height of elegant fashion. "Carolina," he thought, "is literally in another world."

Doctor Woodward, as he had predicted, lived barely a month after Tom had sailed from Carolina, and, to the best of Tom's knowledge, Atsego had gone back to the wilderness. The days were long on his voyage to England. Tom's great height made him very uncomfortable in the tiny cabins of the Warwick Castle. Fortunately for him, the sailing weather was good, and Tom was able to sleep on the deck - to the amusement of the Master and the crew. They had been impressed, however, by his agility and balance on the ratlines and shrouds. For a landlubber he had been accepted and liked by everyone aboard.

Now Tom found himself pivoting as he led his partner through the swaying moves of the minuet. "How amazing," he thought, "the way things have evolved."

He had been received by the Beckwiths in such a warm manner that he felt immediately at home. Over the past seven months he had developed a deep fondness for both of them, and he felt that the fondness was reciprocated.

Tom readily understood, at first contact, the meaning of the "polish" to which Henry Woodward had referred. The noise and bustle of the city had, in the beginning, astonished him. Though he had never been lacking in confidence, the actions of ships and people in Plymouth had caused him to feel the confusion and humility of a rustic. London had nearly overwhelmed him, but he soon became familiar with her ways.

The size and intensity of the Beckwith medical practice also caught the young Doctor by surprise. A busy day in Carolina with Doctor Woodward would consist of four or five house calls and, perhaps, ten or eleven patients during surgical hours. Alternating the days with Doctor Beckwith, Tom found he would make fifteen or more house calls, though calls were made by carriage rather than on foot. Thirty or more patients during surgery hours were an average day.

In addition, there was the charity work at the hospital. Saint Bartholomew's was a huge barn of a hospital and very old. Here, Tom was able to take over the supervision of the junior apprentices who cared for the hospital in-patients and, thus, take a tremendous burden from Doctor Beckwith's shoulders. He also was able to gain an extremely valuable learning experience for himself.

There were days when Tom would come home from the operating room covered with blood from amputations, or with the accumulated gore from lancing bubos, boils, or wens in order to release their mordant humors. He was, at first, hesitant in contact with smallpox patients, but soon found out that he was apparently immune. He often looked at the cowpox scar on his wrist and wondered if there could be a connection. He became familiar with plague, the Lues Venera, lice, and many diseases of poverty that he had never seen before. His medical knowledge also became "polished".

Tom was but a short three months in the office before he was permitted to treat Doctor Beckwith's private patients himself, if the patients did not object. By that time, most of the patients knew him and trusted him for his own skill. One of Tom's early patients was Lord Pomeroy. His Lordship had embedded a large thorn in his leg while riding to the hounds. The dexterity with which Tom had removed the offending thorn had so impressed Pomeroy that he took an interest in the young Doctor. They shortly became good friends.

As a result of that friendship, Tom now found himself bowing and turning with Pomeroy's wife at the Lord's Grand Levee. A gentle squeeze of Tom's hand brought him out his reverie and back to the moment.

"La", said the lovely Lady Jane Pomeroy, looking with a flirtatious smile into Tom's tanned face, "I feared for a moment you were about to fly away, and leave me to the none too desired company of Lord Drummond."

"A farthing for Lord Drummond", said Tom. I care not for the man! Fortunately, he does not seem to care for me either. Indeed, on several occasions we have narrowly escaped having a quarrel."

The music had stopped and Lady Jane looked up at Tom and said, "Make sure you avoid him, Tom. He is very quarrelsome and Drummond has a broad reputation as being a bully swordsman. He has, to my knowledge, killed three men in duels. He is also, for some reason, a favorite at the court. If one were fortunate enough to best his Lordship in a duel, there is the Kings new edict against dueling. The winner would face the tower, at least, and might even face the chopping block. Drummond, on the other hand would receive a slap on the wrist."

Laughing lightly as he led her to her chair next to her husband at the end of the hall, Tom replied, "I shall certainly try to avoid him, because you have asked me to do so, but, I must say, he does irritate me." Bowing over Lady Jane's hand, Tom thanked her for the pleasure of her company, and then turned to the disabled Lord Pomeroy.

"I thank your Lordship," he said, "for permitting me the company of your Lady. I trust that soon your gout will ease and permit you, with your ability so much greater than mine, to lead her through these most intricate steps."

Lord Pomeroy answered, smiling as he did, at the compliment. "Would that physicians would be as gifted with their physic as they are glib with their words. If that were true, I would probably rise for the next dance. However there is some advantage in sitting. Had

I been dancing, good Doctor, I might have overlooked that tall and lovely young lady there by the punch bowl, and would not be able to recommend her to your attention. Were I a towering hulk of a Doctor, I would certainly wander over there. Methinks the lass could almost look eye to eye with you. I will tell you that she has a husband. Lord Faversham, I believe is to become a Governor, or something, in the Colonies. She would probably like to talk to you."

Still chuckling at Lord Pomeroy's quip, Tom worked his way through the people to the punchbowl. Drawing a cup of the sparkling punch, Tom turned and looked at Pomeroy's tall "Beauty".

A beauty she was, and Tom soon found she was as gracious as her lovely serene look indicated. "How wonderful", she said with a smile when Tom approached her, " to find another man, beside my husband, over whom I do not tower."

Tom laughed and introduced himself to this friendly woman, Lady Mary Faversham, who seemed to be in her mid thirties.

Lady Mary said, "Ah, Doctor, your name and fame are well known to me. You may not be aware of it, but these past two weeks my husband, Lord Howard Faversham, has done little but sing your praises."

As Tom raised his eyebrows in question, she continued, "Good Doctor Mac Kaye, for nigh on a year now our favorite groom, Samuel, has suffered from weariness, swelling of the legs, and just general dropsy. Howard told me you treated him with a concoction of powdered foxglove. Since he has been on this medication, after passing much water, Samuel has lost the puffiness of his face and the swelling of his legs. Really ", she said, looking with great sincerity into Tom's eyes, "Samuel, in a matter of a few days, was his active, amiable self again. Truly, Doctor, you have done wonders with him." She would have gone on, but suddenly she frowned and said, "Oh dear!"

The obvious distress in Lady Mary's face and voice caused Tom to turn and look behind him. He saw approaching them a painfully thin, but handsome, man of such height, equal to Tom's own, that it could only be Lord Faversham. Faversham's face wore a serious, worried look. Lady Mary laid a trembling hand on Tom's arm for support, and cried out softly, "Oh I do hope that Howard has not quarreled again about colonial policy. Lord Drummond is such an egotistical dueling bully, and Howard, poor dear, is a statesman, not a warrior."

Scalpel And Hatchet

Striding purposefully, not far behind Faversham, Tom saw the blocky figure of Lord Drummond. Drummond was red faced and obviously angry. Apparently there had been words between the two men.

Faversham had barely reached their presence, when Drummond grasped him by the shoulder, saying at the same time," Now then Sirrah, I demand satis....."

Before the word "satisfaction" could clear the burly Lord's lips, Tom instinctively stepped forward, as Faversham was spun around and out of his way, and slapped Drummond across the face with the back of his hand. The result of the blow was most ludicrous. Drummond, caught unaware, was thrown backward by the force of Tom's unexpected blow. Staggering, he attempted to regain his balance, and, in so doing, he thrust his arm to the elbow in the punch bowl. The bowl promptly tipped and doused him from the waist down. Tom, looking at the dripping, enraged Lord, immediately burst into laughter.

The room rang with Tom's laughter. A dead silence had fallen over the rest of the assemblage. They were all aware of Drummond's fearsome reputation. Drummond, face livid with rage, roared, "You clumsy colonial lout! You shall answer to me at dawn tomorrow, and you," with a snarl, he pointed to Faversham, " will be next, when I am finished with this bumpkin!"

"My Lord", spoke up the pale Faversham bravely, "I should be first, not second."

Still smiling, Tom gently pushed the white faced young Lord back near his Lady saying as he did, "Milord, we may not have the opportunity to spend much time together in the future. This, itself, is sad for I would fain like to know you and your Lady better. Nonetheless," he added in a loud voice that could be heard in every corner of the room, "Milord, were I you, I don't believe I would be in a hurry to rise so early as the dawn. There will be no second confrontation tomorrow, for I thoroughly intend to relieve this company and, indeed, the world of this tiresome, quarrelsome bully and I mean forever!"

There was a soft sigh and a ripple of movement among the onlookers. Drummond's face was blank. No one had ever challenged him so boldly.

Looking directly into the suddenly concerned face of Drummond, Tom continued, "Since I seem to be the challenged, I'll choose the weapons. My favorite weapon is the hatchet, but I fear Lord

Drummond would be too cowardly for that, and he would be sure to say that the hatchet is not 'a gentleman's weapon'."

Pouring coals on the fire, Tom added with a sinister smile, " but, I trow, I have never considered Lord Drummond in the category of a gentleman."

Suddenly pale, Drummond started to speak but Tom cut him off, saying, "I suppose it will have to be swords or pistols. I would dearly love to deflate him and teach Lord Drummond some manipulations with the sword, but, alas, too often a man will get a scratch with a sword sufficient to draw a drop of blood and observers say that 'honor is avenged'. Since I intend to kill you, Lord Drummond, pistols it will be."

With a grim smile Tom added, "In my vocation as a physician one tries to save the patient, though sometimes you bury him. I have no intention of saving you, Lord Drummond. I intend to bury you!"

Lord Drummond, a wrinkle of doubt upon his forehead, was silent.

Early the next morn as the blackness of night was graying into dawn; a gentle breeze seemed to blow the gathering light into the open space on the forest edge where the principals of the duel were assembled. The grass underfoot was wet with dew and wraiths of mist, like ghastly ropes, twined through the trees. The seconds were talking on the edge of the dueling ground, inspecting the pistols, and arranging the details of the combat to come. Drummond, once again confident and haughty, was standing to one side. He was dressed in the regimental uniform of the Royal Brigade. Not knowing Tom's fencing ability, Lord Drummond was quite satisfied with pistols. In the event that he eliminated Tom, as he was sure he could, he had savagely insisted on the sword for Faversham. It was well known that Faversham was inept with weapons.

Lord Faversham, standing nervously to one side, while waiting for his turn, should it come, was formally dressed in a morning coat, breeches, and a lace choker. All of the other principals were dressed similarly, save for Drummond in his regimentals, and Tom. Tom was plainly dressed in riding clothes and boots, and his black hair was pulled back in a neat club.

Doctor Beckwith, who was acting as Tom's second, came over to where Tom and Faversham were standing. "Tom", he said, "We're about ready to begin. In any event, if the outcome is as you have predicted, the law will be after you. We've already said our farewells, and you will not have a moment to waste. The Master of the Wayfarer is already rigged for sea and standing at anchor in the channel, ready to sail. He will have a boat waiting for you at the pier until mid afternoon. Your belongings, sent last night, are already on board. Your horse, saddled and ready to go, is tied to that tree near the coach. Since we will probably never meet again, good luck, and may God bless you. Remember, should you kill or wound the Lord, tarry not. The King's edict against dueling might bring a slap on the wrist for a Lord in the King's Royal Brigade, but, as an example, they would probably hang a colonial. So, be gone quickly, and God speed."

Faversham added, "Good Luck!"

Tom, without appearing to be looking, had been watching Drummond carefully. He did not trust the man. When the duelists accepted the pistols from their seconds, Tom took notice of the shiftiness in Drummond's eyes, and the look on his face. He knew that Drummond had a plan, and a thoughtful look crossed over Tom's face as they stood back to back, waiting for the count to begin. When the director began to count, Tom took the steps, but at the tenth count, he turned left rather than the more natural movement to the right, and well that he did. Drummonds pistol roared before the count was barely finished as Tom was making his turn, but Drummond's dishonorable shot missed because of the left turn. Looking at the Lord, now visibly shaking, Tom spoke coldly as he raised his pistol, "A black-hearted, dishonest poltroon to the end!" and shot him through the heart.

Drummond collapsed to the ground.

The Lord had barely fallen, when Doctor Beckwith was at Tom's side. He grasped Tom's arm and cried, "Tom, to horse, to horse! The word is out and," pointing to a cloud of dust down the road, he continued, "Even now the King's riders approach!"

Quickly Tom shook Beckwith's hand, and with a wave to Faversham, Tom ran to the waiting horse, untied and held ready by a footman, vaulted into the saddle, and started at a gallop down the road to Plymouth. The King's riders had already tired their horses and shortly gave up the chase.

While they were gone, Doctor Beckwith said to Faversham, "We would be well advised to remove ourselves before they return. Were I you, I would hurry my plans for the Colonies!"

Chapter IX

The three hundred ton brig Wayfarer, Plymouth to Philadelphia, tossed the last salt spindrift high into the air from her bow, and drove into the estuary of the Delaware. River. The sun rode barely above the morning horizon and, seemingly, threw the shadow of the giant standing at the ship's rail over the whole of the land. The first gust of land breeze brought the cool, clean smell of his homeland to the nostrils of the man. The breeze cut through the smell of salt, decay, and fish, and bore with it the clean, clear tang of evergreen. Doctor Thomas Todd Mac Kaye filled his lungs with air and gazed eagerly at the green land of his birth.

At the dock Tom was referred to an Inn a few blocks away and well within walking distance. Leaving his chest to be sent on later, Tom carried only his precious instrument case and a small necessity bag to the Inn. As the door to the Crown and Sixpence swung closed behind, Tom paused for a moment to survey the tavern room before him. Oddly enough, he stopped there in the shadow in almost the exact spot where his Godfather, Atsego, had stood on the day of his birth.

A small fire intermittently glowed and smoldered in a blackened fireplace, merely enough to take the edge off the early spring chill. A small group of men sitting around a heavy oaken table at one side of the room nursed their tankards as they listened to a sweating, red-faced man, who was declaiming in a loud voice "the obvious ineptitude of Parsons and others of his ilk! " Across the room the owner of the Inn, clad in his simple leather apron, was engaged in filling a tankard from a wooden keg that was standing on a crude plank bar.

Ducking his head to avoid the low hanging, smoke blackened beams above him, Tom walked over to the landlord, as the curious eyes of the drinkers gazed speculatively at the tall, young, and well dressed stranger.

"I am Doctor Thomas MacKaye", said Tom, extending his hand to the landlord, "and I would like to lodge with you until I can find more permanent quarters. I intend to open my practice here in Philadelphia."

"Glad we are to have ye here at the Inn, and also in the Colony," answered the landlord, shaking Tom's hand. "New faces build the Colony, and a physician is always sorely needed".

The landlord paused and looked past Tom, nodding toward the men at the table and said, "Already Doctor, it seems as if Major Batesford would have words with you."

Acknowledging his thanks to the landlord with a smile, Tom turned and found the red-faced speaker from the table standing directly behind him. This was obviously the aforementioned Major Batesford. Before a word was spoken, Tom could not help but take an immediate, instant dislike to the man. It was apparent at a glance that Batesford was belligerent, arrogant, obviously wealthy, and not a little drunk. The breath that issued from the mouth of his sneering red face reeked of the rum he had been imbibing. His scarlet uniform was speckled with the droplets of his drink.

Raising his eyes in a questioning manner, Tom looked down at the man and said politely "Major Batesford?"

"Aye", blared the man, "I'm Batesford. Did I understand ye to say ye're a Doctor or are ye just another of these quacks that let blood, have no training, and know nothing?"

The rudeness of the man rankled Tom, but without letting his feelings become apparent, he replied calmly. "A physician and surgeon I am. I am Doctor Thomas Todd MacKaye. I was apprenticed, almost from childhood, to my Godfather, Doctor Henry Woodward, in the Carolinas. For the past few years, I have served as assistant to Doctor William Beckwith in London, and served as a staff physician at Saint Bartholomew's Hospital. I think that my training can speak for my qualifications."

"Parsons lay claim to more than that", sneered Batesford, as he wiped his sweating face with a fine cambric kerchief, "but, if ye claim to know aught of malignant fever, I'll have ye look now at my niece, though It's damned little I'll be expecting!"

Turning his back on Tom, whose face was nearly as red from anger as the Major's was from drink, Batesford stepped back to the table. Draining his tankard, Batesford spoke to his cronies at the table. "Come now men and we'll see if this fellow knows aught of his trade. If he doesn't, we'll run him right out of Philadelphia."

Shaking with rage, Tom started for the Major, but a firm hand held his elbow restraining him. In a soft voice the Innkeeper whispered, " Doctor this is a bad start but," he continued seriously, "the Major is the King's own representative in the Colonies. He can make it impossible for you to continue here, if you cross him. Obnoxious though he may be, go with him and do your best. At any rate the lass, his niece Nancy, is a fine young woman and deserves your attention."

For a moment Tom stared blankly into the kindly, concerned eyes of the Innkeeper. Then, with an effort, he shook himself and felt the cool splash of reason quench the fires of his temper. His recent departure from England was a good reason not to draw the displeasure of the King's representative here. With a quirk of his lips that could be construed as a smile, though for the moment not trusting himself to speak, he nodded his thanks to the Innkeeper. Then he picked up his instrument case and followed the Major and his tipsy friends out the tavern door and into the street.

As is common in the spring, the late afternoon sun, hanging barely above the western horizon, gave no warmth to ward off the damp chill of the wind and the wetness of the ground. Tom regretted for a moment the warm coat he had left behind in the Crown and Sixpence, when he felt the bite of the wind. He was able to shake off the coldness by striding briskly after the Major and his friends. Shortly, the group turned in at a handsome brick house sheltered by a magnificent oak tree. As Tom reached the walkway that led into the house, he was forced to step around a sleek bay horse tethered to a hitching post at the entrance to the walk. Tom was cursing to himself the circumstance that had brought him here, but even then, he was feeling the rising excitement as he realized he was about to attend his first patient in Philadelphia.

With his first glance across the room Tom could see that the golden haired girl, lying in the huge walnut bed, was desperately ill. Her eyes had dark, violet circles and were sunken deep in their orbits. The bedclothes were heaving with her chest as she struggled for breath. The scarlet flush of her cheeks bespoke the fever raging within. Her hollow cheeks and the agonized columns of the long muscles in her neck cried out mutely to the physician for relief.

Batesford had pushed forward and was saying, "Her fever came..." when Tom thrust him aside, saying coldly as he did, "Get out of my way and out of the room, you pompous fool." What the Major spluttered, Tom did not hear. He hastened to the side of the stricken girl. Grasping the wrist of the maiden with his left hand, Tom brushed the wisp of blonde hair from her forehead, and felt the heat of her brow with his right. The girl's thready pulse was thin and barely palpable, and almost too rapid to count readily

Quickly Tom pulled down the coverlet and laid his ear against the girl's chest, not even conscious of the firm breast that pressed against his head. He could hear her heart hammering against the chest wall. It was as if there was a contest between heartbeats and agonized breaths to see which might smash through the rib cage.

At this moment a hand jerked Tom upright, and Batesford's voice boomed, "What the devil do ye think ye're doing!"

Rising with a sinuous, twisting movement, Tom gave the Major the full force of his powerful arm and sent the man staggering back against the wall. With a snarl, the Major produced a pistol from his waist, but Tom had already turned back to his patient.

Smiling into her anxious eyes, he said to her, "Open your mouth as wide as you can. I'm going to use this flat blade to push down your tongue. The stretching of your mouth will probably hurt your sore throat for a moment, but I have to have a look in there."

Obediently, the girl opened her mouth, straining to get it wider. Tom inserted the wide flat spatula and pressed down on her tongue. He was barely conscious of the angry voice of Batesford against the wall and the growling voices of his friends now crowded in the doorway. The physician was unaware of the menacing tones. Already he had seen the grim picture of the dull, gray membrane to the back of her throat, almost completely occluding the trachea. It was the dreaded "Cynache Trachealis"! It was no wonder the lass was battling for each precious breath. The combination of the membrane and the rapidly swelling edema of the throat would soon close entirely the tiny air passage that remained.

In an inspired moment, the boyhood memory of his encounter with the deer deep in the Carolina swamp, flashed through Tom's mind. He clearly visualized the hatchet flying across the clearing and the gash in the neck of the deer. In his mind, he could almost hear the hiss of the air emanating from the almost bloodless hole in the neck of the deer as it lay dying. Without a pause, the memory was transported into action.

Tom had never heard of any physician who might have cut into the trachea, the windpipe, of a living person. A glance at his patient, now deeply in a coma, told him, that while she would probably succumb to the toxins of the fever anyway at a later time. It was certain from the blueness of her lips and the tortured whistle of air through her mouth, that she would certainly strangle in a few moments.

Without hesitation, Tom reached into his instrument case and produced a scalpel. This brought a murmur of approval from the onlookers. "He's going to bleed her", said a voice.

Indeed, Tom did intend to draw off a good pint of blood as soon as he had an opportunity to do so. His thoughts were racing ahead. He could foresee a cantharidin blister over the throat to draw the humors, an enema, and a heroic dose of calomel. Before this, first things first, she must breathe!

Snatching a quill pen from the bedside desk, Tom quickly stripped the lacy barbs of the feather from the shaft. Then he cut a piece of the hollow shaft, open at both ends, about three inches long and having a dull point. Now the preparations were complete. Tom faced the moment of truth, the words were long ago written. "Life is short, the art is long, the occasion instant, decision difficult, and experiment perilous!"

Taking a deep breath, and with some trepidation, Tom leaned over his patient and began his radical and dangerous experiment. Lightly, his scalpel inscribed a thin red line, only an inch and a half long, directly over the mid-section of the trachea. The unconscious girl barely stirred. Her only reaction was one thin hand plucking lightly at the bedclothes. Reversing the scalpel and probing the incision with the blunt end of the handle, Tom noted that the cut barely extended through the epidermis.

Vaguely, he heard one of the onlookers murmur, "He's going to bleed her from the neck. It's the area closest to the inflammation."

Still using the scalpel handle, Tom gently teased the soft tissue aside by blunt dissection. Then with the thumb and forefinger he carefully spread the edges of the wound, all the while feeling the pulsating beat of the carotid arteries beneath his fingertips. With a tag of clean linen Tom carefully sponged the crimson droplets from the edges of the almost bloodless opening and there exposed to view was the glistening, whitish sheen of the cartilage and membrane that formed the "windpipe".

In the momentary pause that preceded the next irretrievable action, Batesford's heavy hand dug into Tom's shoulder even as the bull voice of the Major blared again, "Ye damned scoundrel! Ye're not bleeding her! What knavery are ye about!"

Already tense and nervous because of the enormity of his task, Tom, without looking around, drove his elbow into the Major's burly torso and sent him reeling back again against the wall.

There, Batesford fell to the floor shouting all the while, "Stop him! Stop him!

The quack's going to murder the lass!"

With only a cursory glance at the raving Major and the now menacing crowd surging in the doorway, Tom now leaned over his patient. Stretching the membranous tissue between two cartilaginous rings of the trachea, he deftly slipped the tip of his scalpel blade a half an inch into the trachea. The memory of his experience so many years before with the deer in the swamp was immediately rewarded with a loud "hiss" as the girl inspired the air. Without a pause in his movement Tom slipped the quill tube into the incision, and glanced up at the face of the girl.

For the space of an instant, her respiration seemed easier. Then, to his horror, she struggled to raise her head from the pillow. Her eyes opened for a frantic second, and rolled up into her head, until only the whites could be seen. With that, her body convulsed and she collapsed limply back onto the bed. One hand slid slowly, and finally, over the side of the bed. Sighing in disconsolate despair at his failure, Tom started to rise. Only then did he become aware of his own danger of an imminent and violent demise.

As if in a dream, the bewildered Doctor gazed at the violently belligerent men who were charging across the room toward him. Fortunately, they were crowded and stumbling over one another. A thunderous roar of a pistol, the smell of powder and the crash of a ball, as it whistled past his ear and smashed into the bedpost, brought his stare to the smoking pistol in the Major's hand. The stinging pain on his cheek from a splinter off the life saving bedpost, brought him to his senses.

Without thinking, Tom hurled his opened case full of instruments into the faces of the onrushing men. Then he turned and, shielding his face with his arm, he threw himself out the precious glass window. Even as he landed on the velvety grass lawn, covered with shards of glass, but unhurt, he could hear the women in the house screaming, "Murder, Murder!"

There was no time for the Doctor to reflect on the inanities and insanity's of man. Another pistol ball thudded into the ground beside him. Leaping to his feet, Tom sprinted down the walkway. The bay horse, alarmed by the din, pulled nervously at the hitching post. Blessing the person who had tied a slipknot in the reins, Tom jerked them loose and vaulted into the saddle. The saddle, evidently a woman' saddle, was small, and not too tightly cinched. Nevertheless, Tom kicked the horse in the flanks and began to gallop down the street. Behind him he could hear the rising clamor of the bloodthirsty crowd as they ran for horses to take up the pursuit. The few citizens still on the street in the gathering dusk gaped at the fleeing physician as he raced past.

Ahead of him on the street Tom could see the Crown and Sixpence, separated by a narrow lane from the livery stable on the far corner. Swerving the horse in a wide arc, Tom began to take the corner at a full tilt. He was just entering the haven of the lane when a pistol ball raked the back of the now frantic horse. Lacking stirrup support, the startled leap of the horse sent the Doctor flying over a tremendous pile of manure, which he cleared easily, alongside the stable. With a stunning impact Tom slammed into the side of the stable and fell, dazed, between the wall of the stable and the manure pile. Meanwhile, the horse, pained and panicky, galloped on into the gathering darkness.

Chapter X

"I've got to get out of here", thought Tom, "These people are drunk and crazy!"

He forced himself to lie quietly next to the stable until the hue and cry had passed his hiding place as they all pursued the almost invisible, and riderless, horse. After a few minutes when all of the pursuers had disappeared into the darkness, Tom slipped around to the back of the stable. He paused next to the lighted rear door of the building adjacent to the stable. Risking a quick glance around the edge of the open door, he found himself looking into a store of general merchandise. The store was empty of people save for the proprietor, a short, rotund, balding Quaker.

Without hesitation, Tom stepped silently through the door, unseen by the Quaker, who was looking out the front door searching for the cause of the noise. Tom saw a skinning knife on a shelf inside the door and picked it up. In a trice he had a hand over the Quaker's mouth and the knife at his throat. "I have no desire to do you violence," whispered Tom in the man's ear, "but I am driven to desperation by my circumstances. If you make any noise, I may have to harm you."

"I am a man of peace", said the Quaker. When Tom had removed his hand from the Quaker's mouth, the man added, in a matter of fact, calm voice, "Thou wouldst be the Doctor they pursue?"

Then, as Tom released him, he turned and looked the younger man in the eye and asked, "Didst thou murder the lass, as is said? Thy pursuers were shouting that thou hadst killed her."

"Before God", answered Tom, "I did but what I deemed best to save a dying girl. I failed! Perhaps my attempt was dangerous and foolhardy, but were the same situation to arise, I believe I would try the same thing again. As I reflect upon it, there was nothing else that could be done."

Gravely the Quaker nodded his shiny head and said, "I believe thee. Now what can I do to help thee, for thou must indeed flee Philadelphia. Thou must either take thyself aboard a ship, or take thyself to the woods."

Seriously he added, "The ship, I would guess would be best for one from overseas. The forest is not for a newcomer."

"The wilderness is for me", answered Tom. "I may appear too foppish for it, but I was raised by the Tuscaroras. I am not really a townsman. If you can arm me with knife, gun and hatchet, I'll go to the woods and work my way down to Carolina. In here", he continued, throwing his purse on the counter, "is the payment for my gear. Money has no value in the forests so use those monies, which are extra, for yourself. Should I win free, I may send for it at a later date. If I do, I will sign the note with my Indian name, Tawde."

In short order, Tom was equipped with moccasins, leggings, and weapons, but there were no clothes to fit his huge frame. Grinning widely, as he glanced down at his best city finery, Tom said, "It would seem I were better dressed for dinner with the King than to run in the woods, but it will have to do. Now my thanks to you, my friend, and it is time that I depart for Carolina."

"Directly south", counseled the Quaker, "thou cannot go. For thou to reach the Carolinas, thou must first go north, and then to the west to clear the rivers. Philadelphia lies on a peninsula. East and south of us lies the Delaware River, and west of us is the Schuylkill that flows into the Delaware. There will be no escape there for all boats and crossings will be watched, and the streams are all flooded by the spring rains. Thou must head to the north", he continued, "following the Wissahickon until thou canst cross its headwaters. Then thou must go for four or five days of good travel into the mountains to pass around the Schuylkill and yet due west for several more days before thou can turn safely to the south". Continuing further, he added, "When you reach the great river of the Susquehannocks, thou canst follow the river down into the lands of Lord Baltimore and go then from those lands to thy destination".

Now, grimly aware of the wide detour he must make, Tom distributed his weapons on his person, shook the hand of the kindly Quaker, stepped through the door and into the darkness. Carefully he made his way out of the town and plunged into the wilderness, heading north. In the west there was a faint and ominous rumble of thunder.

That first night Tom spent in a stand of pines. He was protected from the light drizzle of rain by a crude lean-to that he constructed out of two forked sticks and a cross rod that he covered with pine boughs. He was awake and away at false dawn. He traveled north and a little west, as the Quaker had advised, until he came to the banks of a stream that was roily and in full flood. This he deemed was the Wissahickon, plunging southward to the junction with the Schuylkill. For a day he followed a forest trail alongside the stream until, at last, he was able to ford the shallower, upper tributaries, and turn in a northwest direction as per the Quaker's instructions. He had heard no sound of pursuit, and concluded that he had fooled them. He felt that he was far ahead of any pursuer.

Chapter XI

For six days Tom traveled north and northwest over streams and mountains and heavy forests. He reveled in his return to a wilderness that he loved. Rapidly the spring in his legs, as well as the lore learned from his Tuscarora teachers, returned to him. He thought often of Atsego. At the end of the third day he knew it was now time to turn to the west. He felt he was clear of any possibility of being overtaken and captured, but the beauty of the country, so different from the swamps and sands of Carolina, delighted him and lured him further. After all, he was in no particular hurry to reach any destination. The vastness of this wild country, so verdant and rich, and with no signs of a living human, intrigued him.

Finally, on the seventh day, a raw spring day with a light fall of snow, he decided he should go no further, and determined to turn west toward the Susquehanna in the morning. He had no intention of following the river down into the Baltimore country as the Quaker had suggested. Since his only objective was to reach Carolina, Tom knew, while the Quaker probably did not know, that the safe, short way to Carolina was not through the settlements of the white man. He intended to strike across the river and continue west until he reached the Warriors Trail, a path unknown to most of the settlers but well known to his Indian teachers. Later generations would name this the Tuscarora Trail.

When the people of the Mengwe came east, the large majority settled in the region of the large eastern lakes, but one tribe, the Tuscaroras, turned south to the Carolinas. Over the years the group known as the Five Nations decimated their Mengwe brethren and more or less absorbed the remnants of those tribes into the Five

Nations. The Tuscaroras, probably because the distance between them aroused no animosity, remained friends with the Five Nations. They maintained occasional contact with their totem brothers in the north by way of a path following the mountain ridges. Tom retained knowledge of this path because the runners who traveled this path had a favorite story for the Tuscarora children. This was a tale of the "Mountain of the Hawks". Here in the fall there would be an assemblage of thousands of hawks gathered above the mountain. In lazy swoops the hawks would soar in the updraft of air that rose along the steep sides of the mountain. Carried high aloft, the hawks floated southward to wherever they went when the snow blanketed the northland. With the trail as his immediate objective, Tom traveled west until he reached the river, crossed it, and continued on over the mountains.

The first dim grayness of morning light seemed to dart along the floor of the narrow steep-walled valley. Finally, the light cast it's dull illumination into the side cove where Tom had made his camp on the previous evening. The cove in which he slept was merely a four-foot hiatus in the high, sheer wall of the canyon. There was a large shelf of granite overhanging that shielded the camp. Tom slumbered quietly by the ashes of the tiny fire that he had used to warm the remnant of the chunk of ham, given him by the Quaker. His once fine clothing was in shambles so he used the useless coat for a pillow. This was as far as the coat would be going.

False dawn faded again into darkness and then the true light fell on Tom's face and roused him. He sat up, stretched, and yawned lazily. Then he came quickly to his feet, suddenly wide-awake. With the breeze drifting down the valley, the sharp yelps of excited wolves some distance up the glen could be heard. Hastily he re-primed his musket with fresh powder, slipped his knife and hatchet in his belt, and stepped over the cold ashes of his fire.

Warily, Tom slowly worked his way along the twists and turns of the steep walled ravine toward the malevolent noises. There was a light snow falling and the wind blew down the ravine into his face, carrying the chilling, spine-tingling sound of agitated snarls and growls. The direction of the wind was fortunate for it tended to cover any noise he might make, and carried his scent away from the animals.

The savage noises were quite loud as Tom approached a slightly widened area of the canyon. Quietly he slipped behind a large outcropping of rock. Repeated erosion and freezing had caused a split in a huge slab of granite from front to back, almost as if a giant cleaver had smashed down through it. Tom found that he could peer through the narrow fissure and see the whole valley before him while remaining almost completely hidden.

The tableau that spread itself before his eyes was one of conflicting forces; tenacity and stamina on the one hand, patience, hunger, and ferocity on the other. At first glance, Tom saw the carcass of a dead wolf lying some little distance from the rock wall of the valley. A broken arrow sticking out of the hide gave a clue as to the cause of the wolf's demise. The shredded remnants of his pelt and the few fragments of bone that were left attested to the hunger of the wolf's brothers and were no recommendation for their kindliness. The three live, slavering wolves sat patiently facing a crevice in the canyon wall.

Seated on a splinter of rock just inside the small crevice, wedged back into the cliff so that the wolves could only attack from the front, was an Indian brave. It was obvious to the onlooker that the siege had been long and that the Indian was exhausted to the verge of physical collapse. Bracing his body with his left leg to carry his weight, the Indian half sat and half leaned on the shard of stone that was his main support. His right leg was propped on a small rock and the twisted shape of the leg below the knee told a mute story of incredible pain, as well as one of tremendous stamina and fortitude. The beleaguered warrior had only a knobby war club and his own indomitable spirit to hold his position. He had no arrows and his useless bow lay on the ground beside him. The wolves sat patiently beyond his reach and waited for the inevitable ending.

Even great courage and physical strength have limits and, as Tom's eyes took in the situation, the scalp lock of the Indian, topped with a broken, bedraggled feather that dangled down, bobbed down as the exhausted man's chin touched his chest. In a flash the wolves were all on their feet. The largest wolf began to glide, his belly close to the ground, toward the dozing figure in anticipation of the kill. As the wolf gathered his hind legs under him, preparing to spring, Tom slid his musket into the crack, and his shot bowled the wolf over, even as its spring started. With knife in one hand and the hatchet in the other, Tom vaulted over the rock. The other two wolves, frightened by the musket's roar, and panicked by this charging, able antagonist, fled from the scene. The Indian slowly crumbled to the ground.

John G. McConahy

Satisfied that the animals were gone, Tom, after a quick glance at the still form of the Indian, stepped back around the big slab of rock and retrieved his musket. Quickly he reloaded and primed the pan. Now was the time to see to the Indian. Tom leaned his musket in a handy position while he cut down a sapling about two inches thick. He then cut off a piece of the sapling about two feet long and split it lengthwise. Kneeling beside the unconscious brave, he gently straightened the twisted leg and lashed the flat sides of the sapling to the leg as a temporary splint. That being accomplished, he prepared to examine the man for any further injuries.

The manipulation of the leg evidently had roused the man again to consciousness. When Tom looked up from his work, he found himself being appraised by a pair of shining, coal black eyes set in a copper colored face. The high forehead of the warrior would seem to indicate intelligence. The face was rather square with a prominent, slightly hooked nose. The man's features as he looked at Tom were totally devoid of emotion. Physically he was stocky and powerfully built. Tom could guess that he would be a dangerous adversary.

For a long moment the two men eyed each other speculatively. Finally, the Indian spoke in the guttural tongue of the Mengwe, "White man, though you cannot understand me, my life is yours and we are forever brothers".

The Indian's face broke into a large smile when Tom replied in the same tongue, "I am honored when I am called 'Brother' by a warrior of the Ho-de-no-saunee. I am called 'Tawde', and I am a member of the Turtle Clan of the Tuscaroras. Since I am a man of medicine, I wish to know if your hurts are more than that of your leg?"

"I am called Shikellamy, O white warrior of the Tuscarora. Blood brothers we are from this day, and totem brothers also for I, too, am of the Turtle Clan. I am a Pine Chief of the Oneida. Pausing for a breath, he continued, "My hurts, except for this insignificant cut on my cheek, are all in the leg."

"You are wondering how I came to be in this predicament? By my own stupidity. Two days ago I stood on that ledge above and, looking down, I saw that old dog wolf yonder," he said, gesturing at the remains of the first wolf's carcass, "and I wished to have his teeth for a necklace. As I leaned forward and loosed my arrow that slew the animal, the edge of the embankment under my feet collapsed and pitched me down into the ravine. I lay there unconscious for a few moments and recovered to find that the other wolves, which had fled when I killed the first wolf, had now returned and even then were creeping up to me. When I sat up, they turned and ran, but only for a short distance. I guess they could see that I was hurt and nearly helpless, and so they sat and waited. I too sat and waited, but for what I could not imagine. However, my Orenda seemed not to call for such an immediate ending and so, I sat and waited for that which might occur. You appeared. You seem somehow to be inextricably entwined in my Orenda! I cannot think otherwise."

"My friends, Kakanate and his sister Oneonta, were to meet me at the Standing Rock a day and a half of moderate walking above the Mountain of the Hawks. I fear they may have gone on now without me."

He hesitated for a moment and then, looking down at his leg, he said, "Our Orendas seem to be intertwined, Tawde. Friend, warrior, man of medicine do what you must with my leg."

With a nod Tom turned his attention to the injured limb. Bracing the limb with his left hand, he loosed the binding of the temporary splint and ran his fingers carefully over the break. His inquiring fingers detected a fracture of the bone, more or less straight, across the tibia. The fibula seemed to be intact. Gently he tied a rawhide thong around the ankle and ran the long end around the base of a small tree.

Looking over at Shikellamy he said, "Warrior, I would have you reach behind you and grasp the rock at your head firmly. I will then pull your leg straight and bind it in position with the splint. There will, of course, be great pain!"

Without comment, though he realized the ordeal that faced him, the Indian reached behind him and grasped the boulder firmly with both arms. Then he nodded his head to Tom to proceed. Tom became completely focused on his role as physician. He took hold of the loose end of the rawhide with one hand and, leaning the weight of his body, he slowly pulled. The counter balance was the weight of Shikellamy's body and the Indian's grasp on the rock. The leg finally appeared to be straight visually and Tom's fingers told him the broken ends were in apposition. Quickly, he lashed the thong to the tree, holding the bones in place and, reaching for the two sapling splints, he glanced up at Shikellamy. The muscles of the man's arms stood out like great ropes and the veins twisted across his temples like snakes, but the eyes were calm and unflinching.

The eyelids blinked once or twice because of the sweat rolling down from his brow and into his eyes.

It was but the work of a moment to lash the sapling splints back on the leg to hold the broken bone in position. Tom loosened the rope from the tree and stepped over to a nearby birch tree. With his knife he stripped a full thickness chunk of bark from the tree about two feet long. This he rolled around Shikellamy's leg to make a protective "cast" that he tied in place. Shikellamy, now completely exhausted, lay back on the ground and wiped his sweating face with his hand.

"Will I be forced to walk with a hobbling gait and the bent back of an old man, when it heals," asked Shikellamy?

"No," answered Tom, "the warrior will run the forest with a straight leg, and the stamina of the bear!"

Shikellamy smiled gratefully, closed his eyes, and slept.

Later, after they had eaten, they lay beside the small fire that Tom had built and discussed what the immediate future held for them.

"Tawde," said Shikellamy, "from what you have told me of yourself, it would seem to me that you would do well to take me to Standing Rock. My people often pass that place every few days. One or more of my people will take my helpless body off your hands. Others could guide you westward to the Warriors Trail that will lead you to the lands of our brother Tuscaroras."

"The problem", he continued, "lies in getting me to Standing Rock. Perhaps you should leave me here and go on alone."

"No," answered Tom. "We are thrown together by fate, Orenda if you like, or so it would seem, and together we shall stay. If it were not too much pain for you, I could carry you on my back. How far would you estimate it is to Standing Rock?"

The Indian burst into laughter. "I do not believe, O great bull of the Tuscaroras, that even one as massive as Tawde could carry Shikellamy through the forest and over the mountains, like a papoose, on his back! Wrinkling his forehead in question, Shikellamy asked, "A travois?"

Immediately Tom nodded his head in agreement. "Of course. A travois."

Chapter XII

Tom cut two sturdy saplings to a length of about ten feet and placed the butt ends side by side. He left six inches of the first sturdy branches on the side of each pole. A strong piece of another sapling about four feet long was placed under the branches, so that about six inches of the crosspiece extended about four inches beyond the two long poles. When the unions were lashed into place, the final result was a strong cross brace against which Tom could either push, or pull with a rawhide harness. Two additional cross braces were lashed into place at two and five feet below the first brace. These effectively wedged the two poles about three feet apart. The space between these last two cross pieces was filled by weaving a crosshatch of leather lacing that Tom covered with the dead wolf's hide and tied that in place. When the trailing ends were cut off in matching length so that they could drag smoothly, the travois was essentially completed.

At daybreak, the two men shared the last of the Quaker's ham and prepared to depart. Tom lifted Shikellamy and laid him on the wolf skin bed of the travois. He adjusted the already prepared bindings around the Indian so that, tied down, he would not be bounced off the travois as they traveled.

Tom picked up the crude harness attached to front of the crossbar and adjusted it to his shoulders. The travois with Shikellamy lying on it now stretched at an angle from Tom's shoulders to the two dragging ends nine feet behind him.

Tom soon learned that the harness method was fine for travel on flat ground but the travois was much easier to control on up or down grades if he took off the harness and slipped the front bar of the travois over his head. That way he could hold back going down by gripping the bar. Going up he could push his chest against the bar and control direction by holding the long side poles with his hands.

The first two hours were torture for both men. The route north to Standing Rock, as Shikellamy had outlined to Tom on the previous night, necessitated crossing the mountain range northwest of them and then following the valley beyond to the upper reaches of the great bend of the Susquehanna.

Even the mighty strength and stamina of the giant white man were taxed to the limit before he finally stumbled, his burden dragging behind him, to the summit of the mountain ridge. The descent on the other side of the ridge to the valley below, though difficult, was, by comparison with the ascent, much easier. Throughout his terrible discomfort from the bouncing of the travois, Shikellamy made no comment other than an occasional grunt when the litter end would drop over a particularly large rock or fallen tree, and land with a thump on the other side.

Both men were delighted to find that the valley floor, when they attained it, was heavily wooded and the footing was fairly smooth. Entering the forest, they found themselves in the midst of gigantic, deciduous titans, soaring in cathedral-like majesty high above them. The foliage of these great trees almost completely blocked the blue of the heavens, casting a shaded grayness, and made it nearly impossible for other vegetation to exist. The annual fall of leaves had produced a soft flat carpet over which the trailing ends of the travois dragged easily and smoothly. The dearth of brush made travel along the wide aisles between the massive trunks of the colossi of oak, ash, and walnut a thing of ease after the difficulties of the mountains.

Now with the terrain so dramatically flattened, Tom was able to hitch the harness once more to his shoulders. Leaning slightly into the traces, Tom was able to swing into the ground-eating stride of the woodsman; such a stride seems to gulp the miles with a voracious appetite. Throughout the day, the forest seemed to run on and on, interminably. At last, late in the afternoon, the stately forest giants lessened in size, and, finally, the travelers broke from the cover of the woods into an open section of a valley that extended before them for miles.

Chapter XIII

As Tom paused for a short breather a few hundred yards in the open area, Shikellamy shifted the musket that he had been holding beside him on the litter all day. Rolling on his side, he pointed the musket in the direction of a low cut in the mountain range beyond the valley. The mountain range was partially concealed by the foliage of a small grove of trees nearby.

Shikellamy spoke as he pointed the musket, "There, Tawde, is the pass beyond which lies the river and a short distance above is the Standing Rock. There, if we find not my friends, we can very possibly find a canoe."

Tom straightened his back, stretched his arms, and then wiped the sweat from his eyes with the back of his hand. "Well, we could either camp here or, if we push on, we could be at the top of the pass before nightfall. I would say that our best choice would be to settle for the night on the edge of the open area at the foot of the pass, I… Hark! What is that?"

"Quickly! Over there!" cried Shickellamy, pointing to the nearby grove of trees. A thundering roar seemed to pervade the whole valley. "Quickly! Take cover there!" Recognizing the urgency in the Indian's voice and asking no questions, Tom took off at a dead run dragging the travois behind him. The helpless man on the litter was buffeted unmercifully as the travois bounced and thudded over the rough ground.

When they reached the copse of trees, Shikellamy, his voice breathless and shaken by the beating, cried with urgency, "Now get us behind the heaviest stand of trees in here!"

It was difficult to hear one's voice now because the roar was almost deafening. A haze of dust clouded the valley as Tom peered in that direction. Suddenly he could see a dark wall sweeping toward their position. The dust cloud was rhythmic with the bobbing backs of hundreds of animals. The huge mass seemed about to crash on their frail and tenuous shelter, when the ranks suddenly split and streamed past on either side of their cover.

In the Carolinas, Tom had rarely seen more than four or five buffalo. He stared dumbfounded as the mighty herd of bison pounded past the copse. He was roused from his reverie by a rap on his ankle with a musket barrel. Looking down he found Shikellamy laughing at him.

The Indian shoved the musket to him and said, "If you can recover from your amazement, O great hunter, you might shoot our evening meal before the whole herd disappears down the valley."

Tom shook his head and reached down to take the musket from Shikellamy. With a sheepish laugh he said, " O well rested warrior, I will see that thy belly is filled with meat."

Stepping out from the cover of the trees, Tom picked out a young calf trailing the main herd, and neatly shot him behind the shoulder. Dead before it knew its heart was shattered; the calf took two more running steps, then somersaulted and fell on its side.

The spiteful crack of the musket rang throughout the valley over the fading noise of the disappearing herd. The sound of the gunshot did not go unheard by others in the wilderness for a party approaching the mountain pass from the northeast came to a frozen momentary alert at the unexpected noise. The Frenchman leading the party held up his hand for quiet and caution. Stealthily he led the party toward the area where the shot had been fired.

Meanwhile, Tom, unaware that they were not alone in the area, strode over to the buffalo carcass. Leaning over the calf, Tom drew his knife and cut across the throat to bleed the animal. Then he walked back to his Indian friend. He handed the musket to Shikellamy and said with a grin, "If you can hang onto this, I will try to get you under cover at tonight's camp site near the top of the pass. That is unless you'd rather wait here for the buffalo to return."

Shikellamy laughed. "Get me away from the buffalo if you don't mind."

Tom slowly hauled the travois holding the Indian up near the pass where he found an open area in the towering forest on the mountain. Settling Shikellamy in a comfortable area, Tom shed his shirt and went back down the hillside to the buffalo calf. Working quickly, he skinned the animal and cut out a haunch, a rib section and added the tongue, heart, and liver. All of these, he wrapped in a part of the hide and then, rising to his feet, he slung the bundle over his shoulder. Bending somewhat under the weight, he trudged slowly up the steep hill toward the campsite.

As Tom stumbled up the rough trail, sweat, intermingled with dust, ran from his brow and into his eyes. Though he lowered his head to reduce the flow into his eyes, they were smarting and burning. Doggedly he continued on the path, slitting his eyes so that he could barely see. A stream of blood from his burden ran down over his shoulder and dried there as a bloody grime. The toll of the day's work was taxing even the great strength of the man. Finally, with an effort he staggered into the clearing where he had left his friend. With a sigh he released his burden and let it slide to the ground. He wiped the sweat from his eyes and started to straighten, when a blow to his head drove him to his knees and then the ground rushed up to meet his unconscious face. Shikellamy, bound and gagged, gazed bitterly at the Frenchman, the leader of the Algonquin raiders, who was standing beside the unconscious body of his friend.

Chapter XIV

Jacques Philippe Saint Jean, Sieur de Montmagny, left his home in France for the New World in somewhat of a hurry. He happened to have run some twelve inches of tempered steel through the mid section of one of the King's favorites. That gentleman, the son of a Duc, had over-imbibed, and mistook Saint Jean, obviously, for someone else - someone of lesser ability with a sword. After his arrival in New France, Saint Jean continued to play the part of the dilettante and expert in seduction; the same role that he had enjoyed in Paris.

However, Montreal was not Paris and the Sieur soon tired of affairs of the heart in the Provinces. Restlessly he looked around and soon observed that the major action in New France lay in travel. He further observed, that a person could not very well travel unless one were familiar with the Indian allies who guided and protected the French explorers in their journeys.

Accordingly, Saint Jean moved himself into a nearby Algonquin village and took for himself a squaw. Within a year he spoke the language fluently and had fathered a child. Accompanied by some Algonquin guides he had traveled as far as the shores of the great lake where dwelt the Hurons. These Hurons were Mengwe relatives of the Iroquois, but were allies of the French, and enemies of their Iroquois brothers. He stayed with them for a summer of fishing and hunting.

By this time the Governor in Montreal considered the Sieur as one of the outstanding and most daring of the leaders available to him. It was not surprising then that Saint Jean was chosen to lead a small party into "Penn's Woods" to determine the westward expansion of the English toward the Ohio country. If he were able to cause some trouble between the English and the Iroquois, without suspicion being directed toward the French, it would be an added benefit. Saint Jean leaped at the assignment!

Early in the spring, Saint Jean, accompanied by Francois Vizena and Pierre Leroux plus twelve of their savage Algonquin allies, paddled up the Richelieu and then down the lake named for the Sieur de Champlain. Leaving their canoes at the southern end of the lake, the party crossed over the mountains into the "forbidden" lands of the Iroquois. Hurriedly they slipped across the valleys of the Maquas (Mohawks}, known as "the flesh eaters". From there they followed a small stream down into the mountains of Penn's Woods and on into the valley of the Susquehanna.

In this vast wooded wilderness of the mountains Saint Jean and his companions felt relatively safe from discovery. However, on their second day, they were not fifty feet from a raging stream swollen by the spring rains, when they came upon an Indian maid standing on the bank of the stream. She was looking away from them, but Saint Jean, aware that she might look around and see them at any moment, sprang forward and tackled her. The maiden, stunned and breathless from the bruising attack, was unable to make a loud sound. The muffled noises that she did make were lost in the roar of the water.

Vizena was about to bury his hatchet in her head, when Saint Jean hissed, "Stop, you fool! She's not alone here. There must be a party of Iroquois close at hand. If we kill her and leave her body, they'll be breathing down our necks. Bind her and gag her. Start upstream with her and look for a crossing while I try to make it look as if she fell into the water and drowned. That way they'll be looking for her down the river. We want them to be drawn that way. We certainly don't want them to search up here. They'd spy our trail right away. Go upstream, quickly and quietly. I will follow in a moment. Pray that I can make this convincing. We could all lose our hair!"

As the group, carrying the maiden, started upstream, Saint Jean picked up the maiden's pouch and jacket that were lying on the bank, and also a hand-sized rock. Carefully stepping from stone to stone he worked some fifty feet down the river, leaving no sign. Finally he reached his objective, a large boulder hanging out over the water. There he stepped out on the boulder and dropped the pouch and jacket. Satisfied with their position, he made a skid mark, using the rock in his hand, in a patch of moss on the edge of the rock as if the woman had slipped and fallen into the swift water. Seeing that his scenario was convincing, he retraced his steps and hurried upstream to overtake his party. They could dispose of the woman when they were far away. Until then, she could walk to her place of destiny.

Chapter XV

A guttural burst of laughter, coupled with the searing pain in his left wrist burned sharply through the haze of Tom's consciousness. His head was thumping under the knot that had been raised when the flat of the tomahawk blade had clouted him. His straddled, erect position was uncomfortable and threw his weight on his left wrist, a wrist that seemed to burn with ever increasing fire. Despite all this, Tom stirred not at all while his head slowly cleared.

He was aware that he was standing naked, and that he was tied between trees facing a clearing. The light of a fire danced across his face although he was far enough away from the fire itself that he could feel none of its warmth. An acrid taste of gall arose in his throat. It came not from fear, but from the red fury that was rising throughout his whole being as he realized how he was confined. A rawhide thong around his waist held him against the eight-inch trunk of a tree. His legs were widely straddled - each ankle being tied to two small saplings. Evidently his captors, whoever they were, had initially tied a long leather thong to his right wrist, and after throwing the end of the thong over a tree branch, they had heaved his unconscious body to an erect position, and left his weight hanging on that wrist. Then with typical savage cunning they made two parallel cuts on his left wrist, passed a rawhide thong under the skin between the cuts, and then tied that wrist to another branch.

It was the burning pain of that left wrist that finally roused Tom to consciousness. Tentatively Tom slightly moved the fingers of his left hand. Though there was some pain with the movement, he was relieved. It seemed that the rawhide ran under the skin itself, not under any of the tendons as sometimes happened. With his head still hanging on his chest he gradually shifted his weight onto his feet. Shortly thereafter, his right wrist and hand began to tingle as the numbness of his hand began to recede now that the pressure of his weight on that hand was eased. He became aware that blood from his scalp wound had run down over his chest. Now dried and caked, the blood obliterated the totem mark on his chest. Awake, fully conscious, and alert, Tom cautiously opened his eyes a mere slit so as to see his surroundings.

There were twelve Indians and three white men standing around a small fire, some twenty feet away from the fringe of trees among which Tom was bound. To the right of the fire lay the body of Shikellamy staked out on the ground in a spread-eagle fashion, and evidently still alive. His broken leg, still in the wooden splints, was staked with a slight twist that must have been extremely painful.

Listening to the conversation by the fire, Tom had some difficulty following the language, which was more guttural than that of the Tuscarora, but he was able to gather the sense of their words. He had evidently been captured by a group of Algonquin raiders, led by the three Frenchmen. Evidently, these Northerners had crossed the Iroquois lands as a move to test how stringently the Five Nations were enforcing the Treaty of Montreal. That treaty had been made in the previous century when the Five Nations had hammered the French to their knees. It was apparent from the conversation that the party was about to split, and that some were to return to Canada. The current subject of discussion was in regard to the disposal of their three prisoners.

The mention of a third prisoner brought Tom's hooded gaze to the other side of the fire. There he could see a bound and bundled form. The braided tresses would seem to proclaim a female, a squaw. With his limited vision Tom could only surmise that she was young by the faint gleam of firelight along a smooth firm jaw.

Turning his attention back to the group by the fire, Tom eagerly strained his ears as the tall Frenchman, who by his air of supercilious authority, was obviously in command.

"Francois," said the tall, saturnine leader to a short bearded man, "the Iroquois may or may not have discovered our passage across their lands. If they have, a party may even now be on our trail. Since the commandant at Montreal desires to know how far toward the Ohio Country the English have extended, I will strike over the mountains and the crooked river with six Indians and Pierre to Le Bouef. Then we'll swing north along the lake and cross the river well above the great falls. We shall probably spend the winter with the Hurons and then cross Canada in the spring to Montreal."

"You, Francois," he continued, "are to return to Montreal by a different route than that we traveled. First, though, send four of your men as scouts on the back trail to see if we have been followed. Whether or not we have been followed, you will have to take your chances, but there must be no trace of my party to the west. The prisoners must not be given a chance to tell what they have seen. The squaw, who is healthy and can walk, you may take with you or slay, as you please. The Iroquois with the broken leg cannot travel and probably would not provide much sport for our allies. Just cut his throat and throw the body in the spring floods. It is doubtful that any trace of him will ever be found."

Pausing, he rubbed his jaw as he looked in Tom's direction.

"The white man, though able to walk, is too large and powerful to take with you as a prisoner. Therefore, he must die, but there is no reason for him to die quickly." With a grim smile he continued, "Though the man is strong of frame, you can easily see he is pale and soft with city living. I cannot fathom what he is doing here in the wilderness. Yet here he is and he should provide great and lasting sport for our savage friends. Let the Algonquin make him plead and scream for mercy. I would that I could stay and hear him myself."

Shaking his head in obvious regret, he said forcibly, "But we must be away. Leave the body of the white man where it is when you are finished with him. If the English should find him, they will probably blame the Iroquois or the Lenni Lenape. Either way, it could cause ill feeling and possibly great trouble between them."

The departure of tall Frenchman, together with Pierre and six of the Indians did little to reduce the odds against Tom and his friends. However, when four of the remaining warriors set forth, as ordered, to check the back trail, a glimmer of hope ran through the heart of the captive. Tom remained quiet until he was certain the four scouts were well away from the camp. When he was satisfied they were gone, Tom began to moan softly until he had attracted the attention of Francois. At that point Tom began to cry. So great was the burning anger within him that real tears of rage, misinterpreted by the enemy as a sign of weakness, began to roll down his cheeks. While he cried and groaned in apparent anguish, he worked his toes, leg muscles, and wrists to dispel the numbness of his limbs. Shikellamy and the squaw looked on. He in amazement, she in disgust!

Francois, the remaining Frenchman, laughed at his captive's apparent cowardice and said, "Our little wren is awake. We wouldn't want you to again become so tired that you would drowse away in sleep. We'll just try to interest you enough to keep you awake, and perhaps alive, for a long time."

"Monsieur," he said with a wolfish grin, "I believe you won't drop off to sleep too easily!"

With a snarl Vizena shouted to the two remaining Algonquin's, "Get on into the forest and bring us enough dry wood to char the hide of this weeping lamb, so we can hear him sing a song in praise of our cooking!"

While the Indians disappeared into the forest, Francois knelt down in front of his naked prisoner after scraping together a pile of leaves, twigs, and small branches with the intent of building the opening fire under the straddled arch of the white thighs. Having arranged the dry tinder to his liking, the Frenchman glanced around at the burning campfire, and made a rising turn to fetch a burning brand to light his fire and begin the torture. As he turned, Francois took his eyes off his captive. With that small error, all the berserk wrath of the captive man, now a total savage, welled up within him and burst into violent action!

With one titanic effort, Tom ripped the rawhide thong through the wide strip of skin that held his left arm bound to the limb above him. His mouth sprang open in a visible, though soundless scream as he tore asunder the living tissue of his wrist. The mighty fist, covered with blood from the freshly spurting wound, descended and smashed into the base of Francois' neck. The Frenchman, almost immediately unconscious, slumped toward the ground. He had barely moved when the gory hand struck again with the speed of a snake and buried its fingers into the Vizena's long, curly, black hair. In a trice, the rampant Tawde raised the Frenchman's head and buried his teeth in the hair, holding the head up, and freeing his own right hand. Tom was beyond the taste of grease, and hair, and blood. Quickly Tom reached down and, though hindered somewhat by the flopping flaps of bloody skin, freed the Frenchman's knife from his belt. With the same fluid motion he slit the Frenchman's throat. Opening his jaws, he spat the hair from his mouth and let the dead body slide to the ground.

It was but the work of a moment with the knife to free his other wrist and ankles. Dropping to his one knee, Tom/Tawde became Doctor MacKaye for a tiny space of time. He took that moment to lay the skin flaps into place and wrap them with a piece of the rawhide that had, a short time ago, held him prisoner. He tied a knot using his other hand and his teeth; teeth smeared with grime, gore, and grease. That done, the bestial primitive took over again.

With what appeared to be a single fluid motion to the astounded onlookers, the great white, blood smeared figure bounded to the side of the campfire. He scooped up a hatchet lying beside the fire and, without pause in his movement, silent as a shadow; he glided into the shadow of the forest. Less than a minute later one of the Algonkins entered the clearing bearing a load of firewood. As the burdened figure of the Indian moved into the open area, a white arm swung like an avenging sword. Reflected firelight glinted from the spinning face of the weapon as it flew through the air, and buried itself with a "thunk" of eternal finality in the head of the Algonkin. The white man leapt into the clearing and wrenched the hatchet from the dead Indian's head. He disappeared again into the forest and returned after a very short interval carrying the bloody scalp of the second Indian

For a few moments the nude whiteness stood quietly against the background of the forest, and then stepped wearily over the nearly decapitated body of the Indian/. Kneeling quietly beside Shikellamy, he cut loose the bonds of his friend. With the professional glance of a physician he looked at the torn flesh of his wrist and nodded in tired satisfaction at the wound. The flapping fragments were held together by the rawhide ties and had quenched the bleeding. Looking back at Shikellamy, Tom croaked, "I must rest!" Flopping down beside his friend, he fell into the deep sleep of utter fatigue. Shikellamy took a blanket from the Frenchman's pack by the fire, and quietly covered the frame of his warrior friend. Then he crawled across the clearing and freed the woman.

Chapter XVI

Crystalline beads of water condensed on the surface of an elm leaf and finally combined into miniscule trickles that ran down the leaf veins. They, in turn, joined together to form a drop on the very tip of the leaf. The droplet hung quivering on the point until a faint trace of vagrant breeze climaxed the performance by shaking the droplet free. Down, down it fell until at last it erased its icy existence in a splash on the arm of the exhausted sleeper. Instantly Tom was awake and with a groan, he stretched his aching muscles. Suddenly his mouth filled with saliva as the smell of roasting buffalo meat came to his nostrils, wafted from the fire by the same vagrant breeze that shook free the dewdrop. When he opened his eyes, he saw the young woman smiling at him as she knelt by the fire. Now in the daylight he could see the fine features of her face that were set off by braids nestling softly against her cheeks and curling down to rest on her bosom.

Tom's moment of admiration was interrupted by the voice of Shikellamy. "Oh great bear, we thought you might sleep, as if in winter sleep, until the other Algonkins returned to slit our throats!"

With a laugh for the Oneida, Tom rolled to his feet and groaned again as the aches and pains of his battered muscles and sinews made their protest. Looking first at the laceration on his wrist, the Doctor found that the loose tabs of flesh where the rawhide had torn through the skin were, despite the hurried wrapping, nicely held in position by the lacing and fixed in place by the clotting of the blood. There was no sign of serious or abnormal inflammation. Rising to his feet, Tom walked over to the fire where the Indian maiden was occupied in carving the buffalo liver on a flat slab of bark. Tom took the knife from her hands and cut loose the bindings of his wound.

Then he smiled down into the deep brown eyes of the young woman and said, "Woman of the Hodenosaunee, I am called Tawde by the Tuscarora who are kin to the people of the Long House. First, I would know how you are called among your people. Then I would beg your favor to rinse the dried blood away from my skin and bind my wound with strips of clean cloth."

The steaming bite of dripping buffalo liver that Shikellamy had just carved wriggled dangerously on the point of the knife, as the Indian aimed the blade at his friend. "Tawde", he said, "even as we sit here now, the four Algonkin that back-tracked to cover the trail, may have already turned and could be moving back to rejoin the group. We are in no condition to face four strong and healthy warriors; not even Algonkins. If we knew of a canoe it would be worth the chance of meeting the enemy as we go east to the river. Should we be fortunate to reach the river, we could easily drift down the Susquehanna and, in a day or two, we could find refuge with Sassassoon. With the permission of the Hodenosaunee, he has established a town for the Lenni Lenape in that area."

Sighing softly, Shikellamy continued, "Indeed, going to Sassassoon's town could be the easy way. However the likelihood of encountering the Algonkin warriors eliminates that possibility. Going due west leads only into the deep wilderness. There the enemy could follow and dispose of us almost at their leisure. In the western wilderness there are no villages or people at this time of the year except for the rare possibility of a Seneca hunting party. There is probably no help for us between here and the forks of the Ohio. This leaves only flight to the north or south."

Taking a stick in hand, the Indian smoothed the dirt beside him with his other hand. Then he drew a half circle in the dirt with the open, convex side facing to the west. Making a point inside the circle, he spoke softly as though thinking aloud. "We are here, situated within the great bend of the river. At the point where we are the waters of the Susquehanna lie almost equidistant to the north, east, and south. At first glance the route to the south would be best - for Sassassoon's town is much closer than Onandaga's Castle. If we went south it is possible that we could keep ahead of the Algonkin until we reached the shelter of the Lenape. This may be the way to go, but I will let you choose."

Throwing the stick into the dirt, Shikellamy looked at his friends and added, "Personally, I believe we should go north toward the Long House."

Nodding his head as he spoke his thoughts, Shikellamy continued, "We have the same chance of reaching the river to the north as we have in any other direction. Once there, Standing Rock is not far away. Somewhere along the river and most likely at Standing Rock, we should be able to find a cached canoe, or we may encounter a hunting party of the Oneida or Maqua. Incidentally, this latter possibility will not be lost on our pursuers and may slow them if they fear an ambush. Therefore, I say we should head for the Long House."

Tom and the maiden listened in silence as Shekellamy talked, and when he had finished, they all sat quietly while they considered his words. The fire crackled and a wet log hissed softly in the flames while the man and the woman thought over the choices.

Finally both heads began to nod in agreement, and Oneonta spoke, "Truly Shikellamy", she said, "thou art Swatatomy, the Enlightener. Your words are good." Thoughtfully, she continued, "Our group is lame but not without the ability to move or to cause damage, if we must. Tawde, though wounded on his wrist, is otherwise sound and he is a mighty and dangerous warrior. I would suggest that he might follow the route of the Algonkin scouts until the sun stands overhead to see about where they are. Meantime I will take Shikellamy on his travois and start north toward the Standing Rock. If Tawde should not at any time see the enemy returning here, or if he has not seen them by the time the sun is overhead, then he should cut across the angle between the two paths and overtake us. Either way, we will know whether we have a chance to flee, or whether we should lay an ambush and fight as best we can."

Both men were in agreement. Without further comment they quickly made their preparations. Tom lashed Shikellamy to the travois and handed him the Frenchman's musket, after first making certain the weapon was loaded and ready. Then he helped the girl to slip the yoke of the travois over her shoulders.

Finally he handed the bag of the Algonkin's pemmican to Shikellamy saying, "It is well we have the enemy's dry rations. Unless I miss my guess, we will have neither the time nor the inclination during our flight to dine on hot food, even if we dared to light a fire."

Despite the gravity of their situation, Tom had to smile as he surveyed the odd method of transport. Tom waved to Shikellamy as the maiden hauled the litter into the forest. He called out to them, "Watch for me about sundown."

Then he turned to his right and followed the trail toward the rising sun where the Algonkin were checking to make sure their passage had been undetected. When Tom started on the back trail the sun, like a leering orange eye, was barely peering over the nearest eastern range of hills. For the first hour he ran swiftly along the trail. As the sun climbed higher in the heavens he slowed to a still rapid pace, but with more wary care. When the blazing orb in the sky reached its zenith directly overhead, Tom found himself looking down on the brown, roiled waters of the Susquehanna. The bluff on which he was standing seemed to hang out over the water as an extension from the ridge and formed an excellent lookout for a survey up and down the river.

Upstream, he could see to his satisfaction that the watercourse ran straight north for a few hundred yards and then bent sharply at a forty-five degree angle to the northwest. This made the river the hypotenuse of the triangle, the short way to travel to intercept his friends. Tom felt weary and his wounded wrist throbbed from the swinging motion of his arm as he had run along the trail during the morning.

Tom turned his gaze to the south where he could see the stream flowed in a reasonably straight line for several miles. He had no time, however, to study the lower portion of the stream. His eyes had scarcely swung over the scene when four figures broke out of the brush on the far edge of the river. They were only a hundred paces below Tom's vantage point when they began to cross. Prudently, Tom backed off to the narrow animal trail that followed along the river and ran quietly upstream to the place where the trail and the river turned. He was anxious to intercept his friends. The Algonkins, unaware of Tom's presence, proceeded westward in a leisurely fashion. The sun glared with malevolent heat directly overhead.

Loping along the river path, Tom was thinking furiously as he tried to project some kind of a timetable in his mind for the future. His best estimate was that he had traveled for four hours from the campsite to the river. It was now well past high noon. The Algonkin were returning to the campsite at a pace much slower than his own hurried, though careful, trip to the river. By maintaining a fast trot he figured he should be able to intercept his friends on their northern leg long before the enemy reached the campsite and began their pursuit. The chase could not well begin before sundown. Perhaps by that time the fugitives could be near Standing Rock and, with luck, they might meet a party of friendly Indians.

Tom felt utterly exhausted and his wounded wrist ached but he kept trotting. He nearly missed the trail of his friends as he crossed a rocky flat stone area. Fortunately, the damp underside of a stone that had been dislodged by the drag of the travois caught his eye. He shook his head and the mantle of weariness fell from his shoulders.

Tom drove himself in the fading hours of daylight in a vain effort to overtake Oneonta and Shikellamy, but finally gave up when darkness erased the last faint trace of their passage. Rather than taking the chance of missing them, Tom threw himself down in the tall grass beneath the sheltering limbs of a venerable forest oak. He was quickly wrapped in the much-needed arms of deep, deep sleep. Even as he drifted into the depths, his thoughts pictured in his mind the lovely maiden, Oneonta.

Coincidentally, just a few miles north that same young woman, exhausted by her efforts of the day, closed her eyes and dreamed of an arm wrapped around her that was as gnarled and hard with muscle as the root of the tree against which she lay.

Daylight was bright and hard against Tom's eyes ere he split the lids and forced himself to gaze, hooded by his hand, into the glare of the sun. With the dawning of full consciousness he rose quickly for he knew he was far too late in awakening. Still weary, and striving to satisfy his hunger, he stuffed greasy pemmican into his mouth as he trotted along on the trail. He felt he was close to his friends, but it was well after mid-day when he came upon them. He marveled at the stamina of Oneonta in her ability to have pulled the heavy-laden travois so far. As he burst through the last slashing branches that shielded the banks of a small stream, Tom could see the recumbent figure of the lass lying against the far wall of the brook. Shikellamy lay exhausted on his litter on the bank above. The girl had evidently shoved the travois up there before her strength gave out. Shikellamy barely lifted his head as Tom began to splash across the creek, but Oneonta came slowly to her feet and met the now staggering warrior on the edge of the water.

For a long moment the man and the maid gazed in silence into one another's eyes. Then without a word, the maiden placed her hand gracefully on the arm of the man and allowed herself to be led in stately fashion up the bank past Shikellamy. Shikellamy raised his head and looked at his friends but they were oblivious to his presence. Their world at that moment in time was not filled with fear and danger rather with newly awakened desire and love and the need for quiet respite in each other's arms.

In the early hours of dawn, Tom shook himself and thought to himself, "We must move on. The Algonkin may well be on our trail already."

Oneonta awoke and stretched just a little without opening her eyes. Then with a lithe feline movement, she turned and threw out her arms for the man who had been lying there with her. He had been holding her for most of the night while she slept. Her dismay at his absence shocked her into sudden alertness and she sat up and looked around her. Shikellamy lay on the ground beside his litter. His good leg was drawn up under him and he was sleeping quietly. Oneonta arose and slipped away from the campsite, seeking Tawde.

Without disturbing the sleeping maiden, Tom had left her side and clambered up the short bank of the small stream. He parted the bushes in front of him and stepped out into a small open glade. He crossed to a large oak tree and, standing beside the trunk, he found himself gazing down at the swollen waters of the Susquehanna.

Tom placed his hand on the tree trunk and leaned out at arms length to study the area. The stream ran muddy, swift and appeared to be fairly deep. There was an eddy below where he stood and a ten-foot log was bobbing and turning and going round and round. The splintered stubs of what had once been branches and the barkless sides of the log attested to its long and agonized travel down some mountain stream in season after battering season. The log slowly moved along in endless fashion as if waiting for some watery hand to pluck it willy-nilly from its present harbor and send it rushing once more toward the sea. Thoughtfully Tom looked at the log for a moment and then looked around for a further survey.

Upstream there seemed little of interest, except that far above the river made a slight bend. There it apparently widened and the riffle at that point would seem to indicate an area possibly shallow enough to make a crossing. The green vegetation seemed to be unbroken in a solid sweep of both banks, save for the small open glade in which he now stood. Tom was conscious of a feeling of unease as he realized how conspicuous he would be if he stepped away from the tree. Hurriedly he switched his attention to the only other object in sight that could be of interest. This was a small island some five hundred yards or so below him. In low water it would probably become a part of the far bank. As it was, he estimated the island to be about fifty feet long and thirty feet wide. The island fit into the vague pattern of an idea forming in Tom's mind.

As the big man leaning against the tree was completing his study of the river, he became aware that Oneonta had followed his path through the bushes and across the glade and was now behind him. As naturally as though she had done it every day, the slim maiden ducked gracefully under his arm. Straightening, she leaned her head back against his tanned and muscled chest. For a long moment they stood thus with their faces and eyes to the river. Then, as though to a magnet, their heads turned and the blue eyes of the man and the brown of the maid's captured each other. Slowly, and with a feeling of awe and discovery, he turned her so that she was looking up at him. Oneonta leaned back against the tree with an expression of anticipation. Gently he took her face between his hands and, bending down, he kissed her.

After the promise that seemed to have been expressed in Oneonta's face, the cold absence of response coupled with the firm rigidity of those lips brought Tom's eyes open as though he had been splashed with cold water! Tom looked at her face and found not coldness, but rather complete shocked surprise and utter amazement. Tom was at a loss for a moment. Then as he gazed into her bewildered, uncomprehending eyes that had been so filled with affection just a few seconds before, a gurgling chuckle of glee built up within him, and almost burst through the bounds of restraint as the realization came to him.

Though savage man may place palm-to-palm, cheek-to-cheek, rub noses, lock arms, bow gravely, as well as many other methods of address, kissing is a product of civilization. The custom of expressing affection with the touching of lips was completely unknown and came as an utter shock to Oneonta.

With an effort Tom held back his surge of amusement and, speaking gravely to the lovely girl, he said, "That is the manner of my people in telling a woman how he honors her. Thus he expresses a great feeling of fondness and emotion to her."

Happiness came to the face of Oneonta and she asked, "Does the woman also express her feelings in such a manner?"

"Indeed, yes", answered Tom.

It was a different set of soft and passionate lips that, in a trice, were pressed against his. The women of the Long House were always known for their intelligence, and also for their quickness in adapting to new things! For a golden moment the lovers stood in the shelter of the great tree; eager mouth pressed to eager mouth, breast to chest, and thigh to thigh, locked in the wondrous throes of newly found passion.

How long this might have lasted, and where this burning desire might have led, collapsed in the feeble clack of wood on wood. It was a sound that carried across the water and overcame the rippling sigh of the water. Clearly a paddle had slipped and struck a canoe brace.

There was no sound other than the muffled gasp of the woman when Tom's fingers grasped her shoulder in a spasm of warning. Harshly he flattened her against the bulk of the tree trunk. Cautiously Tom peered around the tree. There was nothing visible upstream except for the brown rolling water, here and there laced with foam, and the lush greenery along the banks. Pushing the woman gently to his left, Tom knelt to the ground staying close to the sheltering tree. He used a small leafy twig that thrust out from the main body of the tree to shield his face.

Movement downstream near the small island he had noted before caught his eye. A canoe carrying four Indians whom he could readily recognize as their Algonkin pursuers, even at that distance, swept out from behind the island. The Indians had evidently camped on the island the previous night. Crouching even lower to the ground, Tom leaned out and estimated that the Indians would land shortly a little more than a quarter mile downstream. According to his rapid calculations, they would land, take a few minutes to conceal their canoe, and then strike directly inland until they intersected the trail of the fugitives. The pursuers were almost on the pursued and time was running out!

Galvanized into action, Tom and Oneonta retreated across the little glade and through the brush to where Shikellamy lay. Scooping up the Indian, Tom swung Shikellamy into a piggyback position and trotted rapidly upstream along the river path until at last he reached the riffle he had seen. There he plunged into the water and waded almost across the ford. Then, urging the maiden to stay close, he waded with all possible speed back downstream. Inasmuch as neither Oneonta nor Shikellamy could swim, the little party stayed close to the bank in knee-deep water, but far enough out so as not to leave telltale signs near the bank. Under his breath Tom fervently blessed the roily condition of the water that helped to conceal their passage.

After a harrowing ten minutes had passed - ten minutes during which they almost expected their pursuers to come leaping out at them - Tom led his puzzled but trusting companions to a point parallel to that where they had started. They were at the edge of the eddy that swirled past the glade where the man and girl had stood a short half hour before. Tom had noted the eddy and the log earlier. Almost in perfect timing the floating log swung slowly directly before them. Leaving Shikellamy leaning against Oneonta, Tom plunged into the deep water and in a matter of seconds had captured the log and pushed it over within reach of the other two.

Now, gesturing toward some of the short stubs on the log that were all that remained of its branches, Tom said, "Quickly grab a firm hold on this side away from the glade. Keep your heads down in concealment behind the log and hang on for your life while I propel this out in the current. This will be our ship to freedom."

Then, smiling with a confidence that he certainly did not feel, he pushed their rude craft into the current and ducked down behind it with his friends.

One of the pursuers came to the bank of the river some five hundred yards below the eddy. To the casual eye of the Algonkin leader, Cheekon, as he glanced out over the river there was nothing to be seen up or down the river except for an old and derelict log floating down the flooded water. Without another thought about the log, Cheekon turned back into the forest and resumed his search.

It was a baffled quartet of Algonkins that had excitedly followed the relatively fresh spoor of their prey only to lose the trail despite an extensive search up and down both banks. The fugitives seemed to have flown away. Meanwhile, those they pursued were safely ensconced in the island camp the Algonkins had vacated a scant hour before. Many miles below the island, the log, buffeted by the rolling waters, floated on to its unknown destiny. In their frantic two-day search of the riverbanks none of the Algonkin ever thought of seeking their quarry on the island. They believed it had never been out of their sight.

By noon of the third day, after a night and half a day had passed without a sound or sign of their pursuers, the three companions decided that Tom should get over to the mainland and scout around. It seemed probable that the Algonkins had given up the chase. In the late afternoon when the sun had dropped below the margin of the western hills, Tom, bending low, eased through the brush and began to wade across the relatively shallow water that separated the island from the north shore. Halfway across the open water, in his haste to get undercover, Tom slipped and fell to one knee. Even as he fell, he realized he was at the mercy of a group of warriors who had stepped out of the screening shrubs in front of him. They stood gazing at him as he struggled to his feet. Gaining his balance, Tom looked at the warriors, some ten or twelve at least, and found that his eyes were drawn to the magnetic figure that stood in front of the rest on the edge of the water.

It was not the man's height, for he was not tall and Tom towered over him. The shoulders of the man were broad, but there were others in the party as well as Tom, himself, who were broader and more burly. Part of the presence of the man was in his eyes, intent stabbing eyes of ebony blackness flecked with dancing particles of iridescence, and part was in the slight hook of the prominent nose, coupled with an air of hauteur and command.

The Indian, obviously a man of consequence, was attired as though for a great ceremony. On his feet he wore soft-soled moccasins puckered in front by the lacings, and there was extensive beadwork stitched on the center top piece. The latter part was easily visible because of the buckskin leggings he wore. These leggings were sewn seam to the front, and the bottoms were curved from front to back, making an opening over the instep that exposed the top of the moccasin and its beaded design. The leggings themselves were decorated with beads and intricately woven designs from porcupine quill. A rather plain buckskin shirt-blouse was made colorful by the addition of an epaulet-like feathered shawl and a tippet adorned with multi-hued beads that hung in pendant fashion about his neck. On his head, this powerful presence wore a tight fitting leather skullcap, the gustoweh, which was decorated with circles of small dyed feathers. These led up to a bone swivel in the crown of the cap from which dangled the imperial feather of the eagle. In truth, this garb was not designed for forest travel. For the most part, the other warriors were dressed in simple leather shirts, caps, leggings, and kilts or breechclouts, as their fancy dictated.

For a long moment Tom and the Indian stared at one another, each one in some amazement, until finally the Indian raised his hand.

Speaking in the language of the Mengwe, he said, "I am Daweenet, a Sachem of the Onandagas, and a Sachem of the Council of Sachems of the Hodenosaunee."

Ignoring his somewhat awkward position in the slippery stream, Tom answered the Chief, "I am called Tawde, brother to the Tuscaroras, who call the Hodenosaunee 'brothers', and I am known as a healer of men. My companions and I have been hard pressed by the accursed Algonkins, and we are sore and weary. We ask Daweenet for the help and protection of the warriors of the Onandaga, and we ask for their aid in returning Shikellamy and Oneonta to the fires of the Long House."

Chapter XVII

Cheekon was furious! He and the other Algonkins had searched downstream and at last Cheekon realized they had been tricked. As he trotted upstream on the east bank path, the picture of the little island on which they had camped just a few nights before seared its picture in his brain. That was the one place they had failed to search, and it seemed obvious to him now that their quarry must be there. The vista of the river and its verdant enclosing banks opened to his gaze, as the stream swept past in a slow, lazy curve. Stopping he raised his hand to halt his companions. There before them was the island and, smiling with feral satisfaction, he noted an evanescent, almost invisible wisp of smoke rising over the island.

The quartet of Algonkins stepped back into the foliage and worked their way along the river until they came to a vantage point just below the island ford. Quietly they sank into the brush and patiently prepared their ambush. It was only a matter of minutes that they waited. Oneonta suddenly appeared on the shore of the island, stepped gracefully into the water and began to wade through the shallows to the bank.

Meanwhile, Tom back on the island felt uneasy as he sat beside the fire. He wished he had gone with Oneonta when she volunteered to fetch the haunch of venison that Daweenet's party had left hanging on a tree across the ford. He barely heard in his distraction the "huhs", and "ughs" of the Indians listening to Shikellamy's story. The story lost little in the telling and Tom squirmed uncomfortably under the admiring eyes of Shikellamy's audience. Finally, a feeling of unease and a vague sensation that something was wrong brought him to his feet. Somewhat shamefaced and embarrassed, he left the fireside and waded across the lapping waters following the maiden. Behind him he could hear the "wahs" and muted chuckles of the storyteller and his listeners.

Tom had pushed through the brush only a short fifteen paces following Oneonta's trail when the sign of the Algonkins' ambush, and pursuit of Oneonta caught his eye. Snatching his hatchet and knife from his belt, with fear in his heart for the girl, the big man began to run swiftly but quietly on her trail.

Oneonta, heart beating happily with her secret thoughts of "her" paleface warrior, walked along the narrow path completely unaware of the enemy who was but a few short steps behind her. Even as she stepped into the clearing and espied the venison hanging from the low limb of a bedraggled elm, Cheekon was upon her!

With a long stride Cheekon smashed his left hand over the girl's mouth and swept her, at the same moment, off her feet with his right. The snarling expression of satisfaction that swept across his face vanished in that same split second. His first glance at the ground of the clearing shocked him as he saw the tracks on the ground denoting the nearby presence of a large body of newcomers. Cheekon's companions reached the same immediate realization. Mishwah, armed with a bow reached for an arrow in his quiver.

All too late! With the sinewy silence of a panther, the figure of a lean, vengeful giant came streaking into the clearing. Tom's hatchet, already thrown, took Mishwah full in the face dropping him. He was dead before his body hit the ground. Without pause Tom slammed into the others and knocked the trio sprawling. Falling with the second Algonkin, Tom drove his knife into the belly of the Indian, ripped, and then tried to swing up onto his feet. The convulsive spasm of the dying Indian's legs tripped the white man during his desperate effort and brought him to his knees. Cheekon, his face twisted with hate and fear, swung his massive war club, spiked like a medieval mace, down upon the head of his vulnerable foe. Had Oneonta been able to grasp Cheekon's arm, she would never have been able to stop the fatal descent of the weapon. She did, without pause, the only thing she could do. She booted the Algonkin solidly in the rump and sent him flopping into Tom's arms. The spike on the club buried itself harmlessly in the soil beyond Tom's head. In a matter of seconds Tom had his right arm around the Indian's neck with his hand under the chin. The left forearm braced the other side of the neck and with a quick twist the loud snap of a breaking neck brought the combat to a close. The fourth Algonkin fled.

Rising to his feet, chest heaving, Tom took the girl in his arms and held her quietly until the rustle of brush brought him back to alert reality. Ready for another attack, he found there was no danger. There before him was Daweenet and the Onandaga warriors. All were staring in amazement at the carnage in the clearing. The expression on the face of each and every man presupposed that the stories of Tawde would be told to the farthest cranny of the Long House.

At last Daweenet spoke, "The last Algonkin's flight carried him directly into our party. He will run no more." I can well understand your desire, as you told us, to follow that other party of French and Algonkins but, when you ask me to lead such a war party, I must tell you that I cannot do it."

Daweenet smiled at Tom's expression and continued, "I am a Rokowene, a Shaman of Peace. When the fifty Shamans of the League, really only forty-eight since the two Mohawk seats reserved for Hiawata and Deganawida are never filled, meet in Council, it is my duty to the Hodenosaunee to think of, and to speak for, peace. Therefore, it would be unseemly for me, by tradition, to lead such a war party."

Rubbing his hand against his thigh, he went on softly, "The Shamans of the League rule the League by absolute heredity within each tribe. Any man who would lead a war party of the Hodenosaunee is usually not a Shaman. It is usually a warrior who goes to the war pole and sinks his axe in that pole. Then he begins a war dance around the pole and sings his war chant in which he tells where he would go and what he means to do. If there are any who would follow such a warrior on such a mission, they will readily join him in the singing and dancing, and he will be the leader."

Dahweenet gazed thoughtfully around the area for a moment and then added as his eye fell on a small sapling, "It is not uncommon, when one is away from the village at a time like this, for a warrior to begin a war dance around a small tree such as that one over there."

Having finished his speech, the Rokowene turned and walked back toward the island. As he waded across the ford he could hear the chilling whoops of a war dance in the vicinity of the small sapling.

Chapter XVIII

And so the chase was underway. It was fortunate for the pursued that, even with a two-day head start, they were moving with stealth and great speed through the lands forbidden to them by the Pact of Montreal. Though they were fairly sure they could pass through to the Ohio territory unnoticed, they had no idea that a pursuit, and a deadly one at that, had already begun.

Saint Jean had led his band along the north bank of the Susquehanna. There the river ran from east to west until the river started the loop that carried its waters to the south. Here they left the river and continued west, traveling steadily from dawn until the darkness made it impossible to follow a safe trail. They lit no fires at night and subsisted on parched corn and honey. Although they had encountered no one on their journey to this point, they were still wary and forcing a hard pace. Lucky it was for them that they had a two-day start for Tom and his party had already cut their lead by half a day.

After descending from a heavily wooded pass that led through the mountains, Saint Jean paused on a fifty-foot bluff that overlooked a wide river. The river seemed to flow to the southwest, as far as he could see. He felt sure this was probably the Allegheni that would flow until it met with another stream and form the Ohio. Looking back he signaled for the Indians to stand quietly where they were and for Pierre to move up with him.

Motioning for Pierre to follow him, Saint Jean crawled to the edge of the bluff where the Frenchmen slid under the hanging branches of a pine tree that overlooked the river. The bell-like screen of pine branches covered the two men as completely as a hoop skirt covers the feet of a woman. Even the pine jays, normally raucous about intruders in the forest, became silent in the trees surrounding them when they disappeared from sight.

Peering out from their concealed position beneath the pine, Saint Jean found he could see a considerable distance, both up and down the river. The overhanging heavy brush on the near side of the river made it very difficult to see that shore, except for one area with huge rocks down river from their position, and a small sandy cove, an indentation formed by a tiny stream that flowed into the river. This sandy cove was directly beneath their sheltering pine tree. The far shore, though also heavily covered with brush was fairly distinguishable along the whole of the river's edge. The waters of the river slid smoothly past where they lay. The only break in the pattern of the banks seemed to be the little cove below them.

Patiently and quietly the two Frenchmen lay unmoving while the minutes passed uneventfully. The forest behind them was alive with its normal sounds; the chatter of the gray squirrel, the squawk of the jay, and the friendly "deedeedee" of the black-capped chickadee. Satisfied at last, Saint Jean was about to crawl out from their protective cover, when a movement, alien to the serenely peaceful scene he had been watching, suddenly stopped his crawling. Around the great bend of the river upstream, there appeared, as if out of nowhere, a large freight canoe paddled by three Indians.

Saint Jean placed a restraining hand on Leroux's shoulder as he eased himself back to his former position under the sheltering pine. The two Frenchmen watched the canoe with incredulous eyes as it slid smoothly down the river and then proceeded to turn in their direction. It was almost as if they were drawn by a magnet, as the Indians drove the canoe directly into the tiny cove and beached it on the sand.

Saint Jean looked over at Pierre and placed a finger to his lips for quietness. He gestured for Leroux to go for their Indians. He shook his head from side to side as he pulled an imaginary trigger, saying in essence "no muskets". Nodding his head, he indicated with his fingers the use of the bow and arrow and the use of the hatchet by a swinging chop of his forearm. The ambush should be as quiet as possible. Pierre nodded his understanding and crawled backward from under the pine and disappeared into the forest. The next few minutes could have only one conclusion!

Scalpel And Hatchet

Saint Jean stood up and looked at the three Delawares lying on the bank below, their bodies feathered with arrows. He smiled with grim satisfaction and mused to himself, "There are really no problems here. Since the few signs remaining from this brief encounter are easily covered for the moment, they will in any event be naturally gone in a very few days."

"It is very unlikely," he thought, " that anyone will ever come to this particular spot in the future by land or water. Turning to Leroux, Saint Jean ordered him to tell the Algonkins to place the bodies in the water and to tie them to the canoe. "We'll float them downstream till we find a shallow island in midstream and then cover them with stones. It's unlikely that anyone will ever stop there. Our tracks will be covered."

Tom and his warriors arrived on the scene only a matter of hours after Saint Jean's party had disposed of the Lenape bodies on a small island and then floated off in the canoe, heading for the forks of the Ohio. They were blissfully unaware of the danger not too far behind them. The efforts of the French party to cover their tracks would have been completely successful if a few days had been allowed to pass. The Onandagas stopped at the little cove and were easily able to read the signs in the fresh attempts to disguise the scene. Thus alerted, the buzzards circling over a small island told an eloquent story.

Ahnemose knelt by the waters edge. Familiar with the territory, he drew a picture in the sand for Tom and the rest of the frustrated group. "This water," he said, "flows down this way and meets the Monongahela here to form the mighty Ohio. The Ohio starts to flow westward but soon makes a great loop north where the river of beavers enters at the top of the loop. There the Ohio turns again to flow west and south."

Pausing for a moment to think, he continued, "The question is, where are the French going? If they continue in their canoe on down the Ohio, we will never catch them. However, there is a good chance that they will take to land near the river of beavers at the top of the loop. If they do that, they have two options. They can go northwest directly across the Ohio Country to the French fort at Pontchartain dutroit, or they could go directly north by way of the Pymatuning and on to the French fort at Neeahgara."

Looking at Tom, he continued, "Our only real chance is if they head for the Pymatuning. We might be able to intercept them there at the Pymatuning. If we leave here and go directly across country to the Place of Peace, we should arrive at about the same time.

Chapter XIX

While the pursuers talked over their options, miles below the canoe was gliding swiftly down river. Saint Jean and Pierre lolled easily in the warm sun. A deer, drinking at the side of the stream, raised his head, curious and unafraid, as they passed. On occasion they would see a beaver or a muskrat swimming. From time to time there was the splash of a fish or they might see a duck flying overhead. It was very peaceful. Other than those moments, the paddlers saw nothing. An occasional flick of a paddle was all that was necessary to hold the canoe straight on its downstream course and let the current carry them.

Saint Jean stretched and broke the silence saying, "I have heard that below this fork where this river meets another the Ohio is formed by that junction, and the Ohio then flows north for a while to a point that is not too many leagues away from the Pymatuning. We shall land there at this most northern point of the Ohio and go from there due west into the Ohio Country. After a day's journey west, we will turn north again and then finally we shall go east to the Pymatuning, pretending that we have come to the area from Dutroit. We can then go peacefully and innocently north along the Warrior's Trail to the lake of the Eries and safely on to the fort at Niagara. Once we have arrived at the fort we can at last breathe easily and rest. We shall probably find that there are dispatches for us at the fort. In any event, I shall write my report and you, Pierre, can carry it back to Fort Frontenac, when you are ready."

That said, Saint Jean motioned for the paddlers to go to the shore. "For the rest of our water journey," he said, "we shall sleep by day and travel by night. At this stage of our most successful journey we do not wish to see anybody, nor do we wish to be seen. Beach the canoe over there and conceal it with branches. We will rest here until darkness falls. The moonlight tonight will provide us with enough light to travel to our destination."

When the first bright star appeared in the night sky and the wraiths of mist rising from the river could barely be seen, they paddled the canoe out to the strong central current. The splash of a feeding fish and the loud "geronk" of a frog on the bank were the only sound that broke the silence of the night.

There were three or four fires on the south bank of the stream as they entered the confluence that formed the mighty Ohio. Saint Jean ordered the canoe to the far side of the river and held its course close to the north bank and away from the fires. Shielded by the shadows of the trees overhanging the bank, they slipped past the forks and into the blackness.

Just as the last glimmer of starlight was overwhelmed by the glorious rays of the sunrise, the party came to the first falls shortly after entering the river of the beavers. Seeing that there was no easy portage, Saint Jean had them land on the west bank at the foot of the falls.

"We could probably get around the waterfall," he said to the group, but I think we have come far enough by water."

They took only their own belongings out of the canoe and threw the paddles into the bottom. Then Saint Jean shoved the vessel out into the center of the stream, and watched with satisfaction as it floated down to the Ohio. How far the canoe would travel down the great river, ten miles or a hundred, he did not know, nor did he care. Anyone who found this "gift" would accept it without hesitation and say nothing to anyone.

Striking out on foot, the Frenchman led his group directly west. The warmth of the morning sun was a pleasant change after the night dampness along the river.

"Ten leagues we go to the west, Pierre, and then we will go straight north to the lake of the Eries. We will by-pass the Pymatuning by a considerable distance. I think we would encounter too many people in the area, and we might have too many questions asked of us."

Pleased with his decision, Saint Jean continued, "When we reach the lake we can turn back to the east and follow the lake shore. Somewhere along there we may be able to barter for canoes or build our own. Then we can cross the narrow end of the lake and get to Niagara that way. Along the way, if we should encounter anyone, we can piously say we are coming from Dutroit. Even the Iroquois, should we meet them, would be indifferent. Now then, this is the last portion of our journey that requires some care."

Pierre grinned and answered, "The Governor will be most pleased to learn that such a trip as ours, can be done with little danger."

Saint Jean led his group at a ground covering, but more leisurely pace for two days to the west before he turned north. In the late afternoon of the third day they intersected a broad, well-traveled trail that ran east and west. Taking great care to leave no mark of their passage, the Frenchman led his party across the trail and into the forest on the north side of the trail. There Saint Jean called a halt.

As the individuals settled to the ground to rest, their leader stood in the center of the circle and spoke to them in serious fashion.

"I am sure that all of you could see the signs on the trail of the passage of many feet. Those signs were fresh." Every one of the listeners nodded their head or grunted an assent.

The Frenchman continued, "Almost all of the signs were of people going from the east to the west, and all were moving as if in some haste. I am sure that this trail is the main route to the Pymatuning, the peaceful hunting ground, and yet everyone leaving when this is one of the best times of the year for the hunt."

Again there was a chorus of grunts in agreement.

Saint Jean was quiet for a moment while he thought and then, musing aloud, he said, "I do not like this. I smell trouble. I can't believe that it has anything to do with us, but we'd better find out."

The words had barely cleared his lips when they heard a shout on the trail to the east, and Saint Jean made a rapid decision. In his party Saint Jean had a Shawnee who had taken a squaw among the Algonkins and had joined the tribe. Because the man had some knowledge of the Ohio Country, Saint Jean had fortunately brought him on this trip.

"Kansamee," he called to the Indian. "Get out and sit along the trail until this next party arrives. Tell them you have come here from up toward the lake and that you are headed for the Pymatuning. Ask how the hunting has been, or anything at all, but get information, if you can. It is unlikely that they will be hostile. In any event we will be ready to take action, if we must. Now out you go."

Kansamee, looking well traveled as of course he was, sat on a large stone along the trail until a party of seven Indians came down the trail moving at a rapid walk. Kansamee stood up and faced the advancing strangers and raised his right hand, palm out toward the leading man, in the universal greeting of peace. Throughout the following meeting, the murmur of agitated voices was audible in the woods though the words could not be distinguished. Saint Jean wriggled with impatience waiting for the conversation to be finished. It was obvious to the observers that something was going on somewhere because the voices were excited and the gestures were many.

At last the talkers broke off the conversation and, with the hand salute of peace, the strangers departed and resumed t their rapid pace to the west. Kansamee stood and watched their retreating backs until they were some distance away. Then he plunged into the woods, ostensibly to any observer, heading back to whence he had come.

Saint Jean could scarcely contain himself for the few short seconds that it took for Kansamee to rejoin the group. "What's going on?" he snapped as the Shawnee ran up to him.

Kansamee, streaming with sweat and his usually impassive face now filled with excitement, almost shouted his answer, "Irakwai in war paint at the Pymatuning!"

The Shawnee was so agitated that it was several minutes before the Frenchman could calm him enough to get a coherent story. The Indians on the trail were Maumees. Though they would have liked to travel farther to the south to their village, they were hotfooting it straight west until they had a sufficient distance behind them before they turned south. They had no desire to go south earlier lest they should encounter those mad Mingos, as they call the Irakwai.

"They told me", said Kansamee, "that everyone, even the fierce Cherokee from the Tennessee, were fleeing. They said that everything had been peaceful and a number of tribes were hunting with no problems. Then two suns ago, a small band of Mingos in full war paint stormed into the Pymatuming. The war party was led by a huge white man. He was also in war paint and his hair was shaven into a scalp lock."

Looking directly at Saint Jean as his shaking voice began to rise, he said, "They told me the Mingos were looking for a party of Algonkins led by two Frenchmen!"

Now, almost completely undone, he stammered, "Unbeknownst to us, they have been on our heels from clear over on the other side of the mountains!"

Saint Jean was dumbstruck! He could feel the hairs rise on the back of his neck and the gooseflesh pop out on his arms.

"What smug fools we have been!" he thought, and he choked out to Kansamee, "How many warriors have they?"

Rattled, he could say no more at the moment.

Kansamee answered, "The Maumees said there were not too many in the original group, but there were many other parties of various Irakwai tribes scattered over the Pymatuning. In a very short time most of those put on the war paint and began dancing the scalp dance. All of the other Indian tribes were leaving the Pymatuning in haste!"

Saint Jean hesitated no longer. Though the setting sun was not far from the horizon, he waved for his men to rise and follow.

"North," he said to them, "without pause until we reach the great lake. We cannot rest or sleep. Already some of the Iroquois will be started north to cut off pathways to the lake and any other trails that lead to the east above the Pymatuning. Soon they will be covering the shore of the lake to cut off anyone trying to reach Dutroit or Niagara. Maybe, even now, someone has followed our trail and could be close behind us."

This will be a forced march!" he snarled grimly. "We are in a race for the lake. We could all lose our scalps and anyone who cannot keep up and lags behind most certainly will. Even if we win the race to the lake, we have great problems. We must somehow get to the other side of the lake to reach Dutroit or Niagara."

With that final word he broke into a trot and the others followed.

Chapter XX

All through that night Saint Jean led his party, trotting with the North Star as a beacon, and continued on through the next day without pause. It was a tired and nearly exhausted group that came to the banks of a river. The sun was hanging in the west as it prepared for its final dip into the sea of night. Saint Jean pointed to the stream and said, "Look!"

A spirit of exultation suddenly ran through the group. Until this moment all of the waters they had encountered ran in a southerly direction toward the Ohio. The water in this stream ran in the other direction. With renewed energy they trotted along the bank for only a short space of time when they emerged from the forest. As the last flicker of daylight was dying they found they were looking out at a huge bay, carved out by the river in ages past. Beyond the bay, the lake waters seemed to extend forever.

"The river must be the Conneaut," whispered Pierre.

"Yes," answered Saint Jean. "And that", he said, pointing to a huge bonfire burning down near the shoreline, "is either a trap, or it might just be our means of escape. Get back out of sight! Pierre, take the watch while the rest of us sleep. Wake me in three hours when it is dark. Kansamee will take the watch then while you sleep and I will explore. We have a decision that must be made before dawn!"

Dawn was an hour or so away when Saint Jean made his way quietly down toward the shore. The smoking fire was now reduced almost to ashes. The quarter moon cast a clear pale light from a cloudless sky upon the land and the lake beneath. An occasional soft "pop" would send a minor geyser of ash and sparks from the

John G. McConahy

graying embers of the dying fire. The lapping noise of the surf on the lakeshore was sufficient to maintain a deep sleep in the blanket wrapped figures around the fire, and to drown out the popping noise made by the fire. It was also sufficient to cover any noise that might be made by a careful intruder and, indeed, there was an intruder!

Saint Jean had already made a wide creeping, crawling circle around the sleeping Indians. Now he was very close, close enough to see no evidence of war paint on the sleepers. He would expect war paint if these were the pursuing Iroquois.

"This," he thought, "is merely an innocent party of Wyandot or Shawnee hunters. Were they our enemies, we could slay them all as they slept. Should one of them awaken we can accomplish that, but precious time would be wasted."

He crawled back to his group.

The fire had been built about a hundred paces from the shore. There at the high water mark of the spring storms there was much driftwood to be used for a fire. The canoes in which the sleepers had traveled were drawn up in the sand down near the shore. The canoes were far enough on the sand that an errant wave would not wash them away, but they were not close to the sleeping Indians.

Saint Jean gathered his group together and led them to the shore of the lake several hundred yards below the sleepers and the fire. Pointing to Pierre and Kansamee, he motioned for them to follow him. The rest of the Indians were to remain where they were. The three men moved silently through the sand along the shoreline until they reached the beached canoes.

Following Saint Jean's hand directions, Kansamee and Pierre picked up a canoe and then followed Saint Jean out into the lake water to knee depth. Saint Jean held the canoe while Pierre and Kansamee went back for a second canoe and then a third. While the Frenchman and the Shawnee towed the canoes through the water to where the rest of their party waited, Pierre, at Saint Jeans direction, went back to the shore. There, Pierre sliced a hole in each of the remaining canoes before he rejoined the party.

The whole episode was only a matter of minutes and it was utterly noiseless. There was only the lulling roll of the waves on the shore. The previous owners, still blissfully sleeping, had left the paddles in the bottom of the canoes. It was not long before the French party had loaded the canoes and paddled out into the first gently rolling waves of the lake. Erie, that snarling tempestuous lake, was in one of her kindly moods as they dug in their paddles and moved briskly toward the still visible but rapidly fading North Star.

Well out in the lake, Saint Jean looked back at the receding shore. To his horror, by the first light of dawn, he saw a large group of figures come bounding out of the trees and onto the sandy beach they had just left behind them. One of the figures was notable because of his height. Saint Jean laughed weakly in relief because he had thought to have Pierre cripple the remaining canoes at the last moment. Turning his eyes to the horizon he urged his paddlers onward until land could no longer be seen. Back on the shore the pursuers howled their frustration, and the sleeping Indians awoke, completely confused for the moment.

The fierce chase had taken its toll on the pursuers too. Sitting dejectedly on the sand, they watched the French flotilla disappear over the horizon. There was only a trickle of smoke rising from the once blazing fire. Those strange Indians who had been sleeping by the fire fled into the forest in absolute panic when they awoke and saw the painted faces of the Iroquois as they ran past their blanketed bodies. Though the war party had ignored them, the strangers had no stomach for any conversation.

Chapter XXI

For a long time Tom stood on the edge of the lake, staring out at the empty waters as if he could draw his quarry back to the shore by the intensity of his desire. Finally he turned to Ahnemose, who was standing silently beside him, and said simply, "We have lost".

Having said that, he stepped into the water. Taking a handful of wet sand, he began to wash the war paint from his face and body. The rest of the party began to do likewise.

Wearily, Tom and his Indian allies started eastward on a broad Gaquagaono, a well-traveled trail along the lake. Tom learned that this lake, called by the white men The Lake of the Eries, named for the tribe that once had lived there, was called Doshowahtecarneodi by the Hodenosaunee.

Their spirits were lifted late in the afternoon when they paused beside the trail for a rest. As they were sitting quietly in an open area, a graceful young doe chose that moment to step daintily out onto the trail and was promptly feathered with arrows. Pemmican gave way that night to a meal of fresh meat, the first in many days, and with full stomachs they all looked forward to a full night's sleep.

As they gathered around the fire in preparation, Tom said to Ahnemose, "I will take the first watch."

The Onandaga chuckled and answered with a wave of his arm that encompassed, by inference, all of the land for miles around, "Nundawaronoga, the land of the Senecas, you sleep now in Hodenosauneega. This is the homeland of the Five Nations. We lie safely in the shadow of the Long House. Even the Cherokee come here at their peril. They would be hounded all the way back to the Tennessee."

John G. McConahy

After five days of travel on the trail that finally had turned north around the east end of the lake, the party came to a fork in the trail. There they left the lakeshore and traveled on the branch going to the east. Now the Indians were excited and their pace quickened. The woodlands thinned and finally ceased when they came to open fields that had been tilled and planted with corn. There before them was a village. A number of huts were scattered around, but the eye taking feature were the other huge buildings. These were the bark-covered long houses for which the Hodenosaunee were known. Dogs and children, women, men, and boys came running to greet them in a cacophony of sound, dust, and general confusion. All action suddenly ceased and silence fell when they saw the white man, towering above the rest, as the party reached the first of the long bark houses.

As the group came closer, the rush coverings of the entry to the long house parted and two majestic figures stepped forth. Both men were much larger than the average Indian. Tom estimated that the taller of the two was almost his equal in weight and within an inch of his height. He guessed their ages to be in the neighborhood of forty. They both wore similar clothing of sleeveless, fringed, deerskin jackets and breeches. Their totems were clearly visible on their shoulders; the wolf on the taller, the turtle on the shorter man. A single eagle feather ran through their scalp locks. Both faces were calm, confident, and unsmiling. The faces were painted with streaks of vermilion, yellow, and black that ran diagonally across each cheek.

The smaller Indian looked directly at Tom and spoke specifically to him. "I am Sonosowah and," gesturing toward the other man, added, "and this is Tehwahnears." The eagle feather in the tall man's scalp lock dipped as he nodded his head.

Tom looked at the pair with a feeling of awe. Now he could understand their proud carriage and the feeling of power that emanated from their persons. These two men were the almost legendary war chiefs of the Hodenosaunee, the Guardians of the Western Door to the Long House of the Confederacy. Although any warrior could organize and lead a small war party, these two were the "Generals" when the whole League went to war, and they would designate the leaders.

Sonosowah turned his head and spoke to Ahnemose. "Is this the white man who is known as Tawde, and does he know the tongue of the Hodenosaunee?"

Tom answered instead. "I am indeed known as Tawde. I am a brother to the Tuscarora, whom you call the 'Shirt People'. The Tuscarora also speak the tongue of the Hodenosaunee. I feel honored to be greeted by the great Seneca War Leaders of the Confederacy of the Long House."

Without taking his eyes off Ahnemose, Tehwahnears pointed behind Tom and said, "The lines have been prepared."

Glancing behind him, Tom could see two long parallel lines of men, women, and boys half formed, stretching back for a considerable distance. Frowning, he looked back quickly to Tewahnears, who continued to speak. "That Shaman of the Onandagas, He Who Combs Snakes from His Hair, Atotarho, has in his wisdom and for his own reasons, declared that the white man must run the gauntlet."

Ahnemose was visibly stunned and burst out, "This brave warrior has been our leader......." but his words were cut off by Tehwahnears.

"No warrior, who is not of our people, no matter how brave, can lead a war party of the Hodenosaunee unless he has proven himself by surviving the gauntlet. Atotarho has proclaimed that this man must do so."

Shocked to the core, Tom stared at the somber faces of the two great War Shamans. Finally he shrugged his shoulders and said, "I have already led a war party and though I may never lead another, I must pay for that one. To say that I am unafraid of the gauntlet would be a lie. However, if the leader of the Council of the Hodenosaunee, the Shaman Atotarho, says I must run it, then run it I will. I know that torture and death are the consequences of failure!"

Sonosowah pointed to the path that Tom must run between the two lines of Indians and said, " We two will stand and wait at the finish line."

Having said that, the two turned and strode majestically away. Tom walked without hesitation down to the starting point. First he stripped to his breechclout and moccasins, making sure that the latter were tightly laced to his feet and ankles. He flexed his legs in preparation for the ordeal and turned to face the gap between the two lines of people, lines that stretched for more than a hundred long paces.

Tom noted that every individual in the lines was armed with clubs and heavy sticks that would be used to beat him and trip him if it could be done. The burning anger that he felt deep within him burst into a flame of absolute rage, when he saw the members he had so recently led in the chase after Saint Jean, falling into various places in the lines. The final betrayal came when he saw his "friend", Ahnemose, standing near the front, waving a huge club in his left hand. He looked at the lines leading up the gradual slope leading up to where the two chiefs stood marking the finish line.

With a yell, Tom suddenly sprinted into the gap at the start. The first blow that was struck was a mild stinging sensation on his back, and then Ahnemose struck him full in the face with a handful of flower petals he had concealed in his right hand. He was still waving the club in the air and shouting encouragement long after Tom had passed him. There followed along the way a succession of light taps of sticks, thrown bunches of grass, and lightly administered whips of reeds. Full of wonder he reached the Seneca Shamans where he stopped, breathless and shaken.

Tehwahnears looked at Tom gravely, and suddenly smiled. He looked out over the crowd that had assembled behind Tom and spoke. "Dahweenet has declared this warrior was special when first he saw him. It is a brave man who dares to try, and a great warrior who survives, the Gauntlet of the Hodenosaunee. Such a man is henceforth a member of the Long House."

"Blood has been drawn," he continued as he pointed to a few drops oozing from a scratch on the Tom's back, "and the warrior is acceptable. Now, who will have him?"

A middle-aged squaw with graying hair stepped forward immediately as if the moment had been staged. "Glad am I", she said, "to have this brave warrior for a son. My other son, Dodonoltar, has been gone for two years. With this new son, my fire can be warm and companionable once more. How would you have me name my new son, Tehwahnears?"

The Chief folded his arms over his chest and spoke in a loud voice so that all could hear.

"He is indeed your son, oh woman of the Cayugas, and may great joy be yours. Under ordinary custom, Sonosowah or I would give a name to this warrior. However, until the coming together of the peoples of the Five Nations at Onandagas Castle, and the subsequent Council of Shamans, he is to be known as he is known now, "Tawde". The wise Shaman Atotarho, "He who combs snakes from his hair", has asked for his own reasons that the name of your son should be decided at Council."

With that unusual statement there was much murmuring and the tall white man found himself the center of the curious eyes of all who were there. Kahnahmoah took her new son by the arm and led the confused man away. She had a twinkle in her eye as she glanced over at the bewildered man who towered above her.

She said, "It is not good for a warrior to live alone without the warmth of a woman to comfort him. We must send you out to slay a deer. You can then present it to the wife of my brother, Ronomeah. She is the mother of an unmarried Seneca woman."

Tom's jaw dropped open in sheer amazement. Events were moving rapidly indeed!

Chapter XXII

The Carolina sun blazed hot and the humidity seemed to hold off any semblance of a breeze. Manson pushed his battered straw hat, fashioned from palmetto fronds, back on his head and wiped the sweat from his brow with his forearm. His eyes squinted in the glare of the sunlight as he looked out over the plowed fields of his plantation. The corners of the mouth in his brown, sun-wrinkled face twitched into a vestige of a smile. He enjoyed watching the small figures, chained together, as they cultivated the fields.

"They ain't as good as the black Africans," he thought aloud, "and the kids are a whopping better than the old ones. The old Indians just lay down and die in despair when you chain 'em. We've gotta get more of the kids. Every planter down here knows that. The Africans just cost too damn much to buy 'em!"

Bending forward a little, he spat on the ground and watched a little puff of dust rise where the spittle hit

"Ed," he said to his overseer standing beside him, "I've got a job for you. We need more Indian workers. We need to get those 'Roras' riled up and get 'em on the warpath again. Talk to some of the other planters. If we can get the warriors on the warpath again we can get most of them killed off. Then we can grab all the young ones and the squaws and put them to work the fields."

Rubbing the ball of spittle into the dust with his boot, he paused for thought and then continued. "Get some men together and hide out over by the Indian village. See if you can't grab four or five kids. Make sure you leave a trail that heads back toward town. We'll have wagons just outside of town to haul them away. Bring them back here and hide them. Any tracks that you leave will be wiped out by the traffic going in and out of town. We may be able to get the 'Roras' to attack the town. That'll get everyone stirred up!"

Ed nodded his head in understanding and left.

Not far away, Atsego sat quietly and looked at the lined face of the Tuscarora Chief, Nachininga. The wrinkled brow and concerned look on the face of the Chief told Atsego there was a serious problem at hand.

"Atsego," the old Chief began, "I sent for you, a Susquehannock, because it is said that you are known to the white men, speak their language, and you are able to travel freely. The old Chief leaned back against the trunk of the tree that gave them both respite from the glare of the sun. After a long pause, while Atsego waited patiently, the elder leaned forward and spoke again.

"As you are, no doubt, aware the Tuscarora are in dire circumstance. The Cherokee press upon us from the west. They are more numerous and powerful than are the Tuscarora. We have great difficulty in withstanding their attacks."

The white settlers press upon us from the north and east. We have already fought one disastrous war with the white settlers. It is apparent that another war with them is inevitable since they continue to steal our children and young women for slaves in their fields. My people, my warriors, wish to take up the hatchet again, but I can see no way in which we could win such a conflict. The end result can only be disaster and destruction of the Tuscarora as a nation."

"All this being true, our Council of Shamans and I have decided that we must leave and the difficult choice is where to go." Sighing deeply, he picked up a small twig and slowly broke it into tiny pieces.

"I have considered the long trip to the northwest, through the mountains and down the Kanawha to the Ohio Country. This would mean moving a whole nation, men women and children, through the mountains. Our left flank would be subject to continual harassment by the Cherokee. It seems to be almost an impossible choice, but we may have to take that chance. In addition, crossing the width of the great river could be a major problem, even if we would be allowed to do such a crossing peacefully. You do, I believe, understand what a terrible move that would be."

Gravely Atsego nodded his head and commented, "Such a move could be done, but I would guess that you would lose at least two thirds of your people under the best of conditions. Do you have another idea in mind? You must have or you would not have asked me to come here."

The old Chief raised his head and squinted his eyes as a ray of sun broke through the leafy bower overhead and flashed across his face. Looking directly in Atsego's eyes he smiled briefly and answered, "Yes".

After a temporary pause for thought, he repeated, "Yes. I have an idea of a sort, but I guess it all will depend on you, Atsego, and on Brother Onas."

Atsego's usually unmoving features showed surprise. "Me", he exclaimed! "Brother Onas?"

"Yes, you and Brother Onas", answered Nachininga.

"Brother Onas," continued the Chief, "holds a vast area of land that stretches west from his city to the forks of the Ohio, north from there to the lake where the Cat People, the Eries, once lived, and then back toward the rising sun to the gap in the mountains near the Wyomissing where the river flows through to the sea. I traveled over all of that when I was a young warrior."

Nachininga gazed reflectively as he faced the far green hills. After a pause he turned his eyes back to Atsego. "We could safely send the Tuscarora people in small sections, following the warrior's trail, up the valley of the Shenandoah and into the lands of Brother Onas {Penn's Woods}. That is, if Brother Onas would give us permission to settle there and regroup."

Hurriedly he continued, his thoughts now spilling from his mouth in a torrent of words. "Even if such permission were only for a temporary stay, it would give us the opportunity to make plans for a possible future safe move elsewhere."

Now it was Atsego's turn to gaze into distant space as he considered Nachininga's words.

"Yes", he answered as he rubbed his jaw thoughtfully, and then continued, "Are you forgetting the Hodenosaunee? You speak the same tongue and you communicate with them from time to time, and you call each other 'Brother'. You must consider that distance often makes friendships, but proximity sometimes brings on suspicion, treachery, and death. Witness the fate of the Cat People. You would be moving onto land that Brother Onas claims to be his; land where the white men would permit you to go, if Brother Onas grants you his permission. However, as you well know, the Five Nations may live in peace with Brother Onas but we, you and I, know that those lands are the domain and hunting grounds of the Irakwai, the people of the Five Nations."

With serious doubt in his voice Atsego spoke on, "Our ancestors all crossed the Father of the Waters together, all speaking the same tongue. The Cherokee, Erie, Seneca, Huron, Cayuga, Oneida, Mohawk, Onandaga, Tuscarora and Susquehannock were, at that time, all one people until we split up and settled in different areas."

Pausing for emphasis, Atsego went on, "The Five Nations destroyed the Cat People and the Susquehannocks. They battle continually with the Cherokee and Hurons. How will they feel about you, the Tuscarora? Having said that, I must agree with you. Your idea is the best for your people at the present time. I will carry your message to Brother Onas."

Chapter XXIII

Though Tom had harangued his new mother at great length, Kahnamoah had serenely gone about her business as though he had said nothing at all. He repeatedly told her, "I have no interest in a strange woman at this time, in my already confused life."

Kahnamoah would merely nod her head as if in agreement. Then she said to Tom, "My son, we have a need for venison in the house. Go then and slay a deer."

Now, as he was cutting up the carcass of the deer he had brought in earlier, Tom glanced from time to time at the three women talking near their ganasote, the simple bark-covered house that was his new home.

Kahnamoah was standing, facing toward Tom, where he was working. She was holding a platter of corn cakes. The two strangers had their backs turned toward Tom. The younger of the two, according to her figure, had evidently brought the cakes as a gift to Tom's new mother. After much effusive head movement between the three, Kahnamoah left the others and walked over to Tom. Kahnamoah smiled at Tom and made a flourish with her hand as she picked up a freshly carved haunch of venison. She smiled again at Tom and walked back to the other women where she presented the venison to the older woman. The older woman accepted the gift of the venison with obvious pleasure. After a rather spirited interplay of words the woman turned and looked at Tom with a long and curious stare. Finally she bowed in apparent satisfaction and walked away carrying her present.

Tom had been watching the procedure with some mystification although it was obviously an exchange of gifts. He was completely unaware that it was the Hodenosaunee custom to have marriages arranged between mothers. Such an arrangement often came as a complete surprise to those who were to be married. They may never before have seen one another.

The veiled young woman who had brought the platter of corn cakes was still there. The corn cakes were sufficient evidence of her cooking ability to satisfy her mother-in-law to be. Leaving a smiling Kahnamoah, the young woman walked back to Tom where she looked up at him and said in a low voice, "My husband", as she removed the shawl covering her face.

Tom was speechless for a moment and then he saw it was Oneonta. His heart jumped with joy when he suddenly realized she was now his wife.

When he was adopted by Kahnamoah, a Cayuga, Tom became a Cayuga. However, henceforth he would be considered a Seneca, for a man becomes a member of the tribe to which his wife belongs. That is the custom of the Hodenosaunee.

Chapter XXIV

Jakob John Kohl, the Quaker owner of the general store on Broad Street in Philadelphia, was a calm and peaceful man. That is not to say, however, that he was a coward or even a neutralist. Indeed Jakob Kohl was a bold, brave, and also a curious man. When the big Doctor, running for his life, had put a knife at Jakob's throat, Kohl had been totally unafraid. He instinctively knew that though the fleeing man was in a hurry and excited, he was not panicked. Therefore, Jakob had felt in no real danger.

Although Jakob Kohl was a calm and peaceful man, he also had times when he became restless. He had had a feeling of restlessness ever since the fleeing Doctor had left his store. He wondered where the man might be? He wondered if he could find him?

He bided his time until finally one morning he said to his wife, "Bertha, I believe I will travel out to the Indian village around Paxtang and see if I can do some trading with them. Thou and thy father can handle the store in my absence."

Despite Bertha's demurrals, Jakob packed a mule high in the air with trade goods and with musket in hand and a huge pack on his own back, he left Philadelphia behind him. He headed west for the villages at Conestoga, then Katamoonchick, and beyond.

The Quaker plodded along on the well-traveled trail for an hour or so, content with his decision. His thoughts finally turned to the strange case of the new young Doctor who had been run out of town. Had he not escaped, he would have been subjected to, at the very least, a tar and feathering.

"I wonder," Jakob muttered half-aloud," where he is now. Maybe he's dead. He did seem to know what he was doing. He only took a few items; flint, musket, hatchet, knife, moccasins, and rawhide. Not much, but it's enough if you know how to use them!"

"It is sad," he continued, "that such a talent could have been killed and might still be dead now. All of this was because he did something new and that was obviously responsible for saving that lovely young Nancy's life."

The pursuit of the Doctor had not lasted long because of the coming of nightfall. When the sullen posse returned to prepare for the morrow's chase, they found to their amazement and chagrin that the Major's niece was breathing nicely through the quill in her windpipe. Her color was good and she was on the road to recovery.

"That poor Doctor," spoke the Quaker aloud, "would have no way of knowing they were no longer after him once they learned the lass had only fainted."

The thought that the Doctor didn't know what a success his radical treatment had produced brought the Quaker to a stop on the trail. "I wonder if I might be able to find him if he hasn't left the area?"

On an impulse of the moment Kohl left the trail and went north into the woodland. He kept thinking, trader that he was, that though they are not considered to be very hospitable to strangers, it might be very lucrative if it were also possible to establish trade with the Five Nations. Then too I might find someone who has news of the Doctor.

Impulses frequently get people into trouble. In Jakob Kohl's case it saved his life!

Only a few miles on the trail behind Jakob Kohl, the recently recovered young woman who had been the subject of his thoughts was happily riding. Nancy Faversham was in high spirits. She was on her way to see her parents whom she had not seen for months. Nancy had come to Philadelphia with her Aunt Lydia filled with excitement. Unfortunately, a few weeks after her arrival she came down with a sore throat and fever. She probably would have died from the disease had it not been for the timely appearance, albeit a short lived one, of the strange new Doctor. The only residual of her illness was a small scar on the front of her neck.

Nancy had barely made her first few tottering steps from her sick bed when the next ship that arrived from England bore a letter for her.

"Oh," she cried out to her aunt the news that the letter contained. "Mother says that they are coming to America. They should be down there in the Carolinas by now. Daddy is to be installed as the new Governor General and I'm to join them there."

Major Batesford, who always referred to his brother-in-law as "That Popinjay", merely snorted, but Lydia Batesford brightened visibly. She would be happy to be relieved of the responsibility of her now healthy and lively young niece.

There was a major problem confronting them. Transporting a young woman from Philadelphia to the Carolinas was not without difficulties. Of course, the easy method would be by a ship, but there were no packets by sea for months. True there were trading vessels between those ports that were close together, but how could a young maiden move from port to port and boat to boat on down the coast. Not only would it be improper, but also pirates had to be considered when sailing in close to the shore.

Short of Aunt Lydia personally accompanying Nancy as a chaperone, the problem seemed almost insurmountable. Then an opportunity presented itself that seemed to be the answer to their prayers. It seemed that a number of traders were going as a large party on the trail to the Conestoga village at Katamoonchik. There they would split up and scatter to various areas of Maryland and Virginia to trade with the Indians. One of the traders traveling with the group was one Arthur Marlowe, well known and reputable, who with his wife and daughter was going to the Carolinas. There, Marlowe had previously established a trading post amongst the Cheraw, Occaneechee, and Keyauwee Sioux. When he was approached, Marlowe promised for a fair figure that he would escort Mrs. Batesford's niece to her destination with his wife for a chaperone before he turned back to his own post. The opportunity was immediately accepted.

There was one slight, but important, misconception. That misconception was of there being a "group" of traders traveling en masse to Katamoonchik. True, there were two groups of fifteen or more in each party, but the other traders were pretty well strung out over the miles of the trail. For example, over one ten mile stretch of the trail, Abel Thomas and five other well-armed men were the leading party. They were followed a few miles back by Jakob Kohl, a single man carrying a backpack and leading a pack mule. Bringing up the rear and several miles behind Kohl was a group consisting of a lone man, Arthur Marlowe, and three women. All were mounted on horse and leading a five horse pack train.

The Shawnee Chief, Opessah watched quietly from his ambush site as the Abel Thomas party rode past. The large pack train did nothing to tempt the Shawnee to attack. He had no desire to tangle with six well-armed men. He was anxious to achieve a rewarding but safe coup before he and his men left the area. Opessah had already moved the bulk of his people from their village on the lower Susquehanna to a place called Chillicothe in the Ohio Country. He and his small party of warriors were the last to leave. They had paused here in the hope of plundering someone.

Opessah's scout had run in and warned that the Abel Thomas party was dangerous, but that there was a single man and mule, both loaded with goods, that would be easy prey. The Shawnee ambushers waited patiently but the lone man did not appear on the trail in a time span that was more than reasonable. Opessah was about to give up and move on when they heard the click of horse's hooves on the rocks along the trail.

Opessah's eyes gleamed with satisfaction when he perceived the weakness of the party coming up the trail toward the ambush spot. He signaled his warriors to make ready. The soft "nocking" of arrows was unheard over the clip-clop of the horses on the trail. The riders were completely unaware of trouble. Marlowe, his wife, and daughter were old hands at travel with horse. They all rode astride the saddle. Nancy, accustomed to a more genteel life, rode sidesaddle.

A shrill war-whoop shattered the peaceful quiet of the forest along the trail and startled both Nancy and her horse. The horse shied and stumbled throwing Nancy to the ground. There she lay stunned, unmoving, and also untouched by the arrows that had missed her as she fell. The three Marlowes also lay unmoving on the trail, their bodies festooned with arrows.

Opessah spoke fiercely to his warriors. "No hatchets! No scalps! No more blood! Quickly before someone comes along, load the bodies on the horses and haul them into the woods."

Opessah himself went to the nearest body, which happened to be Nancy. Finding her alive, he bound and gagged her and threw her up over her saddle. Feverishly the men swept the blood from the trail and spread dust over that which remained. In a few minutes there was no evidence that a sharp eye would notice unless they knew something could be found in that particular place. When Opessah was satisfied, they left. The trail was empty and it seemed as though nothing had occurred.

Several miles farther into the forest Opessah had his warriors dump the bodies and take the scalps from the dead. He looked at the one live woman, hatchet in hand, and her terrified eyes knew her life hung on a thread. Dispassionately looking at her, Opessah finally slipped the hatchet back in his belt and said, "We will take the yellow hair with us and give her to our squaws. She may provide them with great sport. Kill her if she gives us any trouble. If we meet anyone, kill her before they see her."

Jerking his head to the west he said, "Let us go. We have done well; eight horses, firearms, powder, goods, and a prisoner. Let us rejoin our people."

Before he gave the order to move on, Opessah had a sudden thought. Pointing to two of his warriors he said, "Backtrack through the forest parallel to the main trail. See if you can find where that heavy laden, lone man went. If you find him in a place where you can safely kill him and take his supplies, do so, and then quickly follow us."

Chapter XXV

The long trail that stretched from the great falls of the Niagara to the Hudson River passed through the heartland of the Long House. The trail was packed down as hard as stone and was as wide as a cart path from much use. The focal point was Kanatakowa, known to the English as Onondaga's Castle. On this occasion the trail was filled with people. The Mohawks and Oneidas were pouring in from the East, the Senecas and Cayuga from the West. The Council of Shamans of the League was to meet in a general meeting of all of the people. Every person who could attend was on his way to Kanatakowa. Who could know if the meeting was one of routine affairs, or possibly one of great importance? Either way, there would be a great social gathering.

Tom and Oneonta walked happily side-by-side, laughing and chatting with their fellow travelers as they ambled along the trail. At night, and on impulse during the day, they would slip away from the crowd and find some secluded grassy glade where they could be alone and make love. At one spot they stayed by a brook that gurgled its music over a small waterfall and poured its water into a small pool. After two days of relaxing and bathing and loving, they regretfully resumed their journey. Oneonta reminded Tom that he was to be "named" at the Council. After a week of leisurely travel, they gathered with the others at the council fire where sat the forty-eight Shamans of the Five Nations.

By tradition, the Onondaga Shaman, Atotarho, presided over the Council of Shamans. When Atotarho rose and faced the massed peoples of Kanonsionni, the Long House, a quiet settled over the multitude. Every man and woman leaned forward as Atotarho, after a short greeting, began to chant in a resonant voice that carried over the whole assemblage. Holding up a belt of wampum filled with information and history, one of many stored there at Kanatakowa, "He who combs snakes from his hair" began to tell the story of the forming of the League. All listened with great interest for these historical tales about their ancestors were well loved. And so Atotarho began.

"My brothers, harken back many moons, before the time of our father's fathers, and their fathers before them. The Mengwe came from the lands where the sun disappears at nightfall, and then they crossed the snow-covered mountains. After great hardship they traveled across the Great Plains where the buffalo are as plentiful as the blades of grass on the ground. At last, they came to rest on the banks of the Namaesi Sipu, the mighty Father of the Waters. There they stood with the sun at their backs and gazed into the distance across the Namaesi Sipu at the lands of the Alleghans, the Talligewi.

The Mengwe were weary and few in number after their great trek. While the travel worn Mengwe laid there by the river, resting and gathering their strength, messengers were sent across the waters. They sought permission from the Alleghans to peacefully cross their lands and go on toward the rising sun. The answer of the Alleghans was to bring the messengers to the banks of the broad river across from the Mengwe. There they tortured and burned the messengers in sight of their brothers on the opposite shore. The Mengwe messengers died bravely, as might be expected, without a sound.

Meanwhile Mengwe scouts had been sent up and down the river seeking a suitable place to cross. One of those who had gone down river returned with several strangers who called themselves Lenape. The Lenni Lenape too had come from out of the setting sun. The Lenape had also been refused passage by the Alleghans. The Lenape had paused and were resting in preparation for the coming battle, for they were determined to cross the river.

And so the Lenape and the Mengwe joined forces. They withdrew from the river and rested out of sight of the Alleghans until they were ready. When they felt they were ready, the Lenape and the Mengwe both crossed the river under cover of darkness. Battle after battle ensued and when the fighting was over, the bodies of the Alleghans covered the ground like the leaves of a forest, and their bones were scattered from the Namaesi Supi to the forks of the Ohio. The Alleghans were no more! Any who survived fled down the great river and were never seen again.

The two conquerors parted. The Lenape continued toward the sunrise until they reached the great salt waters to which there is no end, and there they settled. The Mengwe scattered. The Cherokee went south across the Tennessee. The Shirt People, the Tuscaroras went south and east, as did the Tobacco People. The Huron went north, passing by Neeahgara and then west once again to the great bay. The Cat People stopped on the shore of the lake. The Cayugas, Senecas, Oneidas, Mohawks, and Onondagas went north and turned east to the forests around the lakes that are like the fingers on the hand."

Tom was excited by the story and whispered to Shikellamy who was sitting beside him, "I have never heard this story before."

Shikellamy, like most of the rest, had heard it many times before. He nodded and continued to listen intently. Tom took a moment to look, but could not pick out Oneonta from the crowd of women, who, like the men, were grouped together.

Atotarho paused and took a deep breath before he continued.

"In the years that followed, there were wars between the different tribes of the Mengwe, and between the Mengwe and the Algonkin. The Mengwe who lived by the lakes like fingers became very weak and feared they might be driven away or slain.

During these times, the warrior, Hiawatha, saw his woman and his children killed in one of these wars. Hiawatha took himself into the woods to live. There he waylaid and killed any stranger who passed his way. Often he would then eat the flesh of his victims.

One day the great Huron Chief, Deganawidah, who had crossed the great lakes in a white stone canoe, came upon Hiawatha's cabin. After climbing on the roof of the cabin he looked down through the smoke and saw Hiawatha just then leaning over a pot of water. Hiawatha looking into the pot saw Deganawidah's face reflected there and thought it was his own. He looked for a moment and then said to himself, "This is not the face of a warrior who would eat the flesh of men", and his life was changed from that instant. A great orator, Hiawatha became the spokesman for Deganawidah.

That great Huron Chief had long wished to form a confederacy of the tribes of the Mengwe, but his own people, the Hurons, would have none of it. Deganawidah was able to convince Hiawatha to travel from tribe to tribe of the Mengwe who lived among the lakes like fingers. He used his eloquence to convince the Nations to stop *their blood feuds and lay down the hatchet. After Hiawatha was able to comb the snakes out of the first Atotarho's hair, he brought all of those Sachems together at a council fire at Kanatakowa . Thus the League was formed!*

Now united, the Hodenosaunee acquired fire sticks from the white heads. Save for the Hurons, those other nearby tribes of the Mengwe, the Cat People and Susquehannocks, were broken as individual tribes. Their people were absorbed into the Long House.

The Confederacy, now strong, drove the Algonkin toward the land of snow and ice. The Frenchmen huddled behind the walls of Montreal and begged for peace. The mighty Confederacy gave them peace and the French and Algonkin swore they would never cross the lands of the Hodenosaunee. Now the only other Mengwe living outside of the Long House are the Hurons in the North and the Cherokee and Tuscaroras in the South. We are only at peace with the Tuscarora."

The glowing coals of the fire reflected light on the faces of the women, warriors, and Sachems as they all listened to the familiar, deeply moving, powerful story of the forming of the Confederacy. A sigh of anticipation went through the audience as, dropping his right arm, Atotarho continued.

"*The first Snake Head lay dying and he sang a death chant. The story therein has been told and retold at many council fires. That part you may know but many have forgotten how it went. The Hodenosaunee, "The People Who Are Better Than Other People" made "women" out of the Lenni Lenape! The hunting grounds of the Agonushioni stretch from the sea to the Father of the Waters and beyond, and from the lands of snow and ice far down into the mountains below the Ohio. This much many of you may know. But most people do not know or have forgotten except for those who are charged with the keeping of the wampum. There is more!"*

Shikellamy whispered to Tom, "I never heard more than this."

Atotarho spoke louder. "Then the dying Shaman, the first Atotarho, told of a prophecy made by Deganawidah that only a few of the Shamans remember."

Having said that Atotarho stepped back.

Honowenato, the keeper of the wampum, now stepped forward as a rumble of undertones ran through the assemblage for the first time, and quickly stopped in anticipation. Tom noticed for the first time that some of the older Shamans and Chiefs were nodding their heads and turning their glances in open curiosity in Tom's direction. Even Shikellamy had an odd look on his usually impassive face. Tom knew it would be a gross impropriety for a newcomer to make any noise until the Shaman had finished. He waited feverishly for the words that in some way apparently involved him.

Honowenato now took up the story and said, "The first Snake Head spoke thus.

The Agonushioni will slowly grow until nearly all of the Mengwe will live in the Long House in the Great Peace. Through many summers and winters, great Chiefs will come and go, until, at last there shall come one who will lead the Long House to its greatest strength. That warrior will be of the Turtle Clan, as was Hiawatha."

Now many heads were turned to where Tom and Shikellamy were sitting. To Tom's confusion, many excited eyes were staring at the turtle totem on his shoulder.

Honowenato continued, "That warrior will bear the name of a weapon. Many there are, who will live because of this man, but blood will be on his hands and scalps will be at his belt. He will cast a long shadow. He will be two tongued like a snake but his voice will be true. Through this warrior the Mengwe will further unite and grow."

The conference was noisy with "Waughs", "Hais", and "Ughs" throughout the audience and as all eyes were focused on Tom, Honowenato stepped back and sat down.

Atotarho stepped forward again and said, "He who has been known as Tawde should now come down."

Tehwahnears and Sonosowah, the war leaders, now rose and walked over to stand on each side of Atotarho. Tom, totally bewildered, stepped down to a place in front of the assemblage and facing the three Shamans.

He exclaimed, "You can't mean to think that I am the prophesied leader. First of all, I am not worthy. Secondly, I cannot fit the description."

Sonosowah raised his hand to quiet the rumble of noise from the crowd. Sonosowah's face was calm, but his eyes were black as coal and glittering with excited interest.

"Dahweenet saw something when first you met. Even then he thought you could be the man!" He continued slowly and clearly enough that all could hear. "Almost all of this can seem to fulfill the prophecy. You are two tongued for you speak the tongue of the

John G. McConahy

white man and of the Mengwe. No man would know you were not the brother of either because your voice is true."

He smiled and pointed behind Tom saying as he did, "Lo, you cast a long shadow. You are a Medicine Shaman, Dahweenet's man for peace. You are also a warrior who has killed and will kill again. You are a white man and you are Turtle Clan of the Tuscarora and now of the Hodenosaunee."

"All of that", said Tom, "is flimsy of itself, and my name is certainly not that of a weapon!"

Now stepped forth the Sachem Tehwahnears. Raising his hand and looking at Tom, his hawk's nose seemed to leap from his face while the shadows flickered and raced across his countenance.

"This," he said, "is the naming before the Council of which I spoke, when first we met. It is in the prophecy that you have already been named. That name is not Tawde, so by what other names are you known?"

Flustered but serious, Tom thought and then answered, "I was born and named Thomas Todd MacKaye, but I am called Thomas MacKaye by the white man."

Tehwahnears shook his head impatiently. "A shorter name" he demanded!

Tom, completely baffled, finally said feebly, "Tom?"

Immediately he knew that was what the Seneca Shaman wanted.

"Hai," shouted the Shaman, as the mutter of the whole assemblage became a roar. "Who, indeed, is named for his own weapon? We, the Hodenosaunee call that weapon Osquesont. Our enemies, who call it by another name, shall feel the sting of that weapon! This warrior is named for the Osquesont. Tomawki, the hatchet of the Hodenosaunee! Hai!"

The whole assemblage of the Five Nations burst into a roar, and the two war leaders, Sonosowah and Tehwahnears, stepped up, one on each side of the bewildered white man. Taking Tom by the arms, they led him away to a secluded place in the forest, leaving the excited crowd behind, saying, "Now we must talk."

Sonosowah began to explain things. "Dahweenet met you first and almost immediately knew you for what you are. Dahweenet told Atotarho, who in turn sent the word to us. When you came before us after the pursuit of the French party, we too recognized you as the warrior of the prophecy. You are well named!"

"Now we must talk with you of our plans for the future of the Hodenosaunee. Our strength will be spread very thin so it is essential that Tewahnears and I should plan for the war predicted by Deganawidah, and also be able to assure the safety of the Long House itself. When the time comes you, Tomawki, the Osquesont, will be the Battle Leader."

Chapter XXVI

Sonosowah and Tehwahnears had no idea of the type of problems that were to arise, only the prediction of the Snake Head that they were coming. The war leaders imparted to Tom that they believed he should use his new prestige to mold the warriors of the various tribes into a single working group. forgetting individual war parties.

Sonosowah pointed out the fact that any warrior could take a red hatchet adorned with red feathers, and walk through a village sounding a war whoop to attract attention. Having thus aroused the attention of the people, he could then go to the Gaanadote, the war post, bury his hatchet in the war post and begin a dance. Other warriors would join the dancing and, finally, he would lead the group away to meet the enemy.

Tom's first task, according to the war leaders, would be to go from nation to nation and village to village. He should talk everywhere to the Pine Chiefs and other leading warriors to convince them that they should keep themselves available for the union of all war parties, and that those war parties would be under his leadership.

Now the traveling and work began in order to coordinate the warriors of the Five Nations. Tehwahnears was to work with the Senecas and their juniors, the Cayugas, at the western door; Atotarho had the Onondagas, Shikellamy had the Oneidas, and Sonosowah would be with the Mohawks when the time came.

From time to time as part of the coordination, Tom and Shikellamy would take parties of young men just under warrior age on a hunt, or to practice the use of their weapons in war games. It was on one such expedition that they came upon the trails of two men who were themselves tracking a single man leading a pack mule. They were immediately interested in possible trespassers. Their party completely surprised and captured the two Shawnee who were tracking the single man. Jakob Kohl, unsuspecting of any danger, they found in a deep peaceful sleep. Tom recognized Jakob as his Quaker benefactor at once.

He said to Shikellamy, "This man knows me and he is a good man. I would rather not have him recognize me now. I'll stay back in the forest", and he withdrew leaving Shikellamy to take charge.

Jakob Kohl had spread out a thick carpet of tips cut from pine boughs over which he had laid his blanket. On that soft mattress fragrant with the scent of freshly broken pine, he had enjoyed a deep sleep. Drowsily he lay in the morning light in a half comatose state, lulled by the twittering birds and other sounds of the morning forest. Suddenly the chatter of the squirrels and the song of the birds had ceased. Kohl was wide-awake, his nerves jangling with the sudden silence. Lying quietly on his side as if he was still sleeping, he opened his eyes a slit. He sensed he was not alone, but who or what was there, he did not know.

Only a short distance from his head he could see a pair of moccasins. Before he had the opportunity to glance further a voice spoke to him.

"You are awake, I know, white man, so sit up slowly and carefully. You have been luckier than you realize up to this point. Do not try to push your good fortune too hard."

Jacob rolled slowly from his bed and sat up carefully. Looking around he found himself in the midst of a group of Indians dressed in deerskin pants and sleeveless jackets. With the exception of the warrior sitting on his heels a few paces away, Kohl could see that the others were young, probably in their teens. None of the faces were painted, but at a motion of the squatting man's hand, four young men dressed as were those around Jacob, came out of the trees around the glade. They shoved two painted warriors, hands tied behind their backs, into the clearing.

The older Indian rose from his squatting position and looked at Jacob saying, "Why were these Shawnee in war paint following you into the lands of the Hodenosaunee, whom you call the Five Nations."

Kohl replied with measured words, "I am Jacob Kohl, a Quaker like William Penn. I am not a warlike man but a man of peace. I live in the City of Brotherly Love. I am a trader and I came here hoping

Scalpel And Hatchet

to exchange trade goods with the people of the Five Nations for furs. In truth, I did not know I was being followed."

The Indian nodded his head in understanding, and absently flicked a fly from his arm before he spoke again.

"I am Shikillamy. We, Tomawki and I, are teaching these young warriors the reading of the forest, the use of weapons, and art of the hunt."

Looking sternly at the Quaker, he continued, "Man of peace you may be, but all trading with the Hodenosaunee is done at the yearly meeting at Wyomissing. Any other traders need special permission."

Jakob Kohl smothered a momentary flash of fear within him and spoke out. "In sooth, I would fain have that permission. Canst thou pass it to me?"

The Indian's teeth glistened as he answered, "You are bold to ask such a question when your hair should already feel loose on your head! Fortunate for you and your trail followers, we are hunting in good spirit: and are merciful."

Turning toward to two Shawnee prisoners and their captors, he pointed a finger and merely growled, nodding in their direction as he did, "Women!"

At once with a glee that was easily apparent to Jacob, the young men fell upon their captives, stripped off their clothing and left the two stark naked save for a loin cloth. Roughly they scrubbed the war paint off the faces of the prisoners with harsh sand. Kohl could see blood oozing out of the sanded cheeks. Then the scalp locks, the pride of any warrior, which dares an enemy to conquer him and take his hair, ware crudely and bloodily shaved off their heads.

Satisfied that the Shawnee had been reduced to woman status, Shikellamy spoke, pointing to the west, "Tarry not. You have one moon. Should the rising sun find you within our reach, you will burn."

The two near naked figures waited no longer, but turned and fled.

And now it was Jakob's turn to face the stern gaze of the Oneida. Jakob was aware that there were more of the young men standing around the periphery of the area. One figure leaning against a tree stood out much larger than the others even though that individual could not be clearly seen because of the brush. Bravely, Jakob stood, legs apart and hands on hips.

Looking directly at Shikellamy, he began, "I have done no wrong, no harm."

The Indian ignored him and spoke to the large figure across the glen, a man he addressed as Tomawki. The conversation between the two was too rapid-fire for the Quaker with his limited vocabulary to follow except for an occasional word.

At last the conversation ceased and Shikellamy, a curious look on his face, turned to the Quaker who stood there awaiting his fate. Kohl could sense a difference as the Indian looked him over with eyes that were no longer cold but filled with interest. Having braced himself for the loss of his trade goods and possibly the same humiliation as that of the two Shawnee, Jakob was thunderstruck when Shikellamy turned to one of the young men.

Speaking slowly so Jakob could follow the conversation, Shikellamy said "Take this man and his goods to the next village where he may trade. Tomhawki asks that he be introduced from village to village. Tomhawki says this is a good and honest man. When you have vouched for this trader at the next village and they have promised in turn to introduce him to the village after that, you may return."

Looking at the wondering Quaker with a face now softened by an appearance of pleasure, Shikellamy spoke words that were like drops of joy in the white man's ears, "You are granted permission, or rather you have been invited, to trade in the lands of the Hodenosaunee. 'He who had been prophesied', Tomaki, the Hatchet of the Long House has spoken for you. Should you ever be questioned, merely state that you are the friend of Tomawki and Shikellamy. Go now with your guide."

Waving aside the blurted thanks of the white man, the Indian quickly disappeared as if by magic, into the forest. Looking around, Kohl saw that all of the young men had disappeared as well. Of the tall warrior who evidently had saved him, and for what reason Kohl could not even vaguely guess, nothing could be seen. The young man designated to be the guide touched the Quaker on the arm and said in friendly fashion, "Come."

Chapter XXVII

When Tom made the long trip to visit the Oneidas and Mohawks, Oneonta, now visibly pregnant but able to travel, would accompany him as far as Kanatakowa and stay in the lodge of Dahweenet, the Onondaga Sachem, until Tom returned. On this one occasion Tom had returned as darkness fell and they had retired as they usually did. It was nearly dawn and the dull light of false dawn was barely able to pierce the gloom of night. Tom lay quietly beside Oneonta in Dahweenet's section of the Long House. Wide-awake, he wondered where he was destined to go, and just what the prophecy really meant. Suddenly the quiet village of Kanatakowa was interrupted by an attack from the French and their Huron allies.

The assault on Kanatakowa at the first light of dawn was stealthy, vicious, and totally unexpected. The first "BOOM" of cannon fire that initiated the attack roused Oneonta and brought her to a seated position in her sleeping robes, dazedly rubbing her eyes. Tom, however, weapons in hand, had already burst out of the shelter of the cabin into the open. He heard the chilling sound of war whoops along the north wall of the village. The cannon roared again and a shell burst inside the village. Instinctively, Tom ran to the south wall, leaped up on the parapet, and slid over the wall in a twisting roll. Crouching down to present a low profile target to anyone on the outside, he scrambled into the brush. When he stood erect and warily looked around him, he found to his surprise that six others had followed him over the wall; five warriors and a boy who appeared to be about ten years old.

Pointing south away from the savage fight that they could hear along the north wall of the stockade around the village, Tom said to his followers, "Quick, quick, we must be gone! We must get out of here before they close the circle around the village. We have much work to do!"

Grasping the boy by the shoulder as they ran, he hissed, "You are to burn a path to Oneniote village for help, but not until we are safely through the circle that will be forming. I will tell you when to start, but take the long safe route. A dead warrior on the direct trail is help for no one. You must get through! Your safe arrival at Oneniote will bring our brothers to our aid. Hopefully, it will be in time!"

With a wave of his arm to his followers Tom plunged into the forest. It was wise that they had made an expeditious departure for fighting developed, almost at once, around the whole perimeter of the stockade. Subsequent attempts by the besieged Onondagas to send runners for help were met by whoops of derision from the Hurons. They danced before the stockade walls, waving aloft the bloody scalps of the ill-fated messengers.

Tom led his little band at a fast trot for several miles on a straight line to the south before he waved them to the west. Then a warrior who was familiar with the area took the lead. Some two hours later, when the whoops of the Hurons and the boom of the cannon could no longer be heard, Tom called a halt.

Pointing a finger at the boy, he said, "Go now to Oneniote. Make haste, but go at a steady pace that will get you there. Have the Cayugas come to our aid and have them send a runner to the Senecas as well."

With that he slapped the lad on the shoulder and the boy took off at a steady dogtrot as Tom nodded in approval.

Once they had seen the boy on his way to the west, the warriors turned to Tom for directions and he waved his arm to the north. The group picked up the pace to a fast lope and held that pace for several hours before turning east. At last they finally gained a position to the rear of the attacking French and Hurons. Once there they moved toward the sounds of the gunfire. Inasmuch as the last few miles had to be covered with great caution, it was several more hours before they could get into position not far behind the cannon. There were a few guards stationed to the rear of the attacking forces, but their concentration was focused on the "BOOM" of the mortar, and the fighting on the edge of the village where the stockade had been flattened. Tom and his Onondagas were easily able to slip past these careless watchers. After a stealthy approach, they were scarcely thirty feet behind the mortar and its unsuspecting gunners.

Peering through the sheltering brush toward the village, Tom could see it was in a shambles. Through the smoke and flame he could see that at least one of the long houses and several huts were aflame. The stockade had been breached in two places by the mortar, and fierce 'hand to hand' fighting was raging in the gaps. Tom could see distinctly, a buckskin clad figure outlined by the flame of the village before him as the man directed the attack in the main gap. When the man turned, Tom recognized Saint Jean. Looking to the left, he easily picked out Pierre urging the Hurons on that flank. Cursing the two Frenchmen under his breath, he turned his attention to the nearby gun and its personnel.

There immediately in front of him were two French soldiers as guards, three gunners, and an officer positioned around the mortar. Tom tapped each warrior on the shoulder and indicated which of the French soldiers that warrior should take when the signal was given. Each time the cannon fired, the gunners would turn away from the acrid smoke that followed the flaming roar and then turn back to the gun again to begin the reloading process.

When all of his men were ready and in position with arrows nocked on their bowstrings, Tom waited patiently for the cannon to fire again. When the mortar fired, he waved his revenge filled Onandagas onto their deafened, half blinded, and unsuspecting prey. The warrior who slew the master gunner cut and ripped off the gunner's scalp and then stood up ready to let out a victorious war whoop. Tom's hand across the mouth of the warrior stilled the noise before it began.

"Later," he said, "but for now two of you put on the caps and coats of the French sentinels. Stand where you can be seen. We need some time before they realize the gun is permanently silenced!"

There were two luckless Frenchmen guarding the supply wagons some two hundred feet away beside a little outgrowth of shrubs that shielded them from a view of the gun. They speedily met the same fate as the gunners. Among these wagons holding the bulk of all of the French supplies was the ammunition wagon filled with bags of powder. Tom picked up a bag, slit it open and let it trickle onto the ground under the wagon. He motioned for his warriors to pick up several bags and carry them for him as he successively opened bags and laid a continuous powder trail back into the woods.

Gathering his group around him, he spoke softly despite the noise of the conflict. "The French would expect that any help for the village would be likely to come from the Oneida first. Circle around now to that side. Wait there for the next firing of the cannon. I will be the one firing the cannon and I will try to hit the enemy with the shell. When you hear the gunfire, make a noisy attack from that side; making sure it is more noise than actual attack. They must not learn how few we are! When I hear your attack, I will then light the powder trail and will join you as soon as the supplies have been destroyed."

While his warriors were working their way around to the side where they were to make their attack, Tom busied himself in reloading the mortar. Once loaded, he lowered the mortar in a way that the angle of fire would probably send the shell right in the midst of the French and Huron attackers. When he felt his men had had enough time to attain their objective on the enemy flank, he fired the cannon and saw with satisfaction that his estimated aim had landed the shell just behind the Hurons surging at the major gap in the wall. The explosion caused pandemonium in their ranks! Tom now put the gun out of further action by effectively "spiking" the primer hole on the cannon. He jammed a stick down the hole and broke it off.

Now the war whoops and firing suddenly arose on the one side of the conflict from the presumed "relief force", Tom ran back to the start of the powder trail that led to the ammunition wagon and dropped his lighted fuse on the powder. Immediately, a burning snake of black powder skittered towards the ammunition cart and the cataclysmic explosion of the wagon brought a momentary silence over the whole field of battle. Then the whoops from Tom's five flankers turned the tide; the French and Hurons fled!

Saint Jean, carried along by the retreating flood of men was able to pause for a moment by the cannon. Glancing down he saw what he thought was a stick broken off in the hole. Momentarily mystified, he leaned over in a sudden movement to look closer. As he bent, a hatchet whistled past his head and whacked into a tree where his head had been. Without pause he turned and ran. Glancing back over the fleeing crowd behind him, Saint Jean saw a huge man some thirty feet away, unable to reach him because of the crowd, shaking a fist at him.

Recognition, a sense of deja vu, came to him immediately. This was the leader of the party who had chased him across Penn's

Woods to the Lake. He thought "My Nemesis! Why?" But there was no time for further conjecture.

Saint Jean knew he had to establish some kind of a rear guard to cover their retreat. The Frenchman was finally able to gather together a small group of soldiers and a few Indians. Later, as the rout slowed and there appeared to be no immediate threat of attack, he was able to attract more to his force and the group was able to provide protection for a more orderly retreat. They reached the Ontario Lake and launched their boats, to Saint Jean's relief, without further incident.

"Evidently," he thought, "the pursuit is not yet organized, or they are not yet strong enough, and fear an ambush."

Pursuit indeed! It was several hours later before any relief parties arrived on the scene of the carnage. The arriving parties were so wearied by the pace they had set to get there that they, in turn, were too tired to chase further after the French. As Tom made his way toward the village wall, picking his way through the bodies of defenders and attackers alike, his heart was now pounding with fear for the safety of Oneonta. As he stepped through the wide gap in the stockade he could see long houses and ganesotes were blown apart and many were burning fiercely. Wounded men, women, and children sat in stunned apathy everywhere. The able bodied were dragging the dead and arranging them in a rough line through the middle of the village.

With a quick glance down that line of bodies Tom's eyes fell upon a familiar figure. A cry of despair burst from his lips. Running over to the crumpled body lying there in the dust, he dropped to his knees and rolled her over. It was Oneonta lying there peacefully in death. An exploding cannon shell had blown a huge sharp splinter from a log. The splinter pierced her heart like a knife and killed her instantly.

Without words, Tom picked up that beloved body and carried her into the forest along the trail they had traveled so happily not long before. In his mind's eye he saw the place she loved so well, the grassy bank beside the stream where they had made love. There she could forever listen to the rippling laughter of the stream.

Chapter XXVIII

Day after day the people sat patiently waiting. No one knew exactly what would happen next and no one dared to interrupt the thoughts of the war leaders. But the whole of the League was aroused and all knew that there would be revenge for the attack on Kanatakowa.

Tehwahnears was about to speak his mind, when Sonosowah tapped him on the arm and directed his attention to the massive, painted figure emerging from the forest. Gone was the grief stricken bridegroom. Instead an avenging panther paced menacingly across the clearing and raised a hand to the War Shamans. The tufted scalp lock, two inches wide, ran from his forehead to the nape of his neck, standing up from the rest of the bald, plucked scalp like the crest of a Roman helmet of bygone days. His face, neck, and shoulders were painted a solid black except for the streaks of vermilion and yellow slashed diagonally across the sides of his face. As the warrior drew closer all could see in the startling, fierce blue eyes a look that boded ill for someone. No more was there a Tawde. Tomawki had returned and in his hand, he swung the red hatchet of war!

The two War Shamans rose as the painted warrior came up to them and stood in front of them, looking each in turn steadily in the face. Each of the Shamans placed a hand on the shoulder of the feral savage. The long wait was over for the war leaders. Their battle leader was at hand. The prophecy was coming true!

"Patience, my friend," said Sonosowah. "It is a time for thinking and planning before we go to war, and we have decided that a war it will be. We have had enough of Aragaritka, the Hurons, and Tionontati. They must be destroyed. No more will we tolerate their presence. Blood will flow, indeed, but such a war will involve all of the Hodenosaunee: Mohawk, Cayuga, Oneida, Onondaga and Seneca. It has been fifty years since such a war council has been held. At that time we burned Rique and Gentaienton and destroyed the Eries. Tehwahnears and I were children then, but we are calling for a similar war to erase the Aragaritka from the face of the earth!"

With a concerned look, he continued, "Therefore, warrior, we ask rather than demand, that you delay your war party. Though the French and Hurons are lacking in supplies, they will have ambushes set for any immediate pursuers, and they will be ready for an attack in the near future."

Tom's thin grin and white teeth split the savage mask as he looked at the Shamans.

"And so say I," he replied. "Our food supply is ravaged. Our habitation in this village is destroyed and we have many dead and wounded. My thirst for blood and revenge must be cooled a little so I am able to aim for total revenge on the Hurons and that damned Frenchman. Nevertheless, we must inflict punishment or they will think we are sleeping, cowardly dogs. Your thoughts about the Aragarita are mine and such action is in the future. For now I believe we should begin the end of the Huron by destroying their eyes, Cahiague, the Huron village on Lake Ontario. They must think we may possibly be content with such 'eye for eye' revenge. Let them relax their vigilance when they think they are safe. The French Fort at Niagara is too strong to attack without cannons, but the Senecas can keep them inside that fort and the Maqua can limit Fort Frontenac when we are ready to go to Lake Huron."

Tehwahnears smiled, if the thin slash of red lips across his grim face could be called a smile, and said, "We three think alike, warrior. I will stay at the western door and the Seneca will be seen in force around the Niagara Fort. The French will see enough that they will not be very interested in going out of the fort. They'll be sure not to leave the gates open. While we do that, Sonosowah and Shikellamy will take the Mohawks and Oneida in force, and destroy Cahiague."

Tehwahnears continued their plans. "You Tomawki will take a small party of Onondagas and look at Fort Frontenac. The fort commands the place where the lake empties into the river to Montreal and the sea. Look over the fort. If you think it might be

Scalpel And Hatchet

conquered easily, return unseen by anyone. Should you think the cost would be too high to attack, harass the fort and keep them from coming out. We shall cut off the traffic of the French and the Hurons on the lake till Cahiague is gone."

Agreement to the plan was quickly reached. Tom found that Shikellamy had been summoned several days before and they all worked together till the sun was sliding behind the wall of land to the West. Their plans were ready. The next morning they split up and went to their respective posts. The "pulling" of the Cahiague thorn from the side of the Long House would begin and end, when as many suns as a man had fingers, were passed.

Within three days the garrison at Fort Niagara was frozen in a siege state. When the first Senecas in war paint were seen on the forest fringe around the fort, a party was sent to warn away anyone coming down the Niagara trail from Lake Erie. Although the Senecas turned the group back, one man had hidden and presumably got through to the lake. The Senecas were in good humor as they looked the other way and let the messenger slip past them.

Chapter XXIX

At about the same time, Tom was gazing across a valley at Fort Frontenac. He quickly decided that the fort could be taken, but that it would not be worth the loss of men that the capture would entail. Although Fort Frontenac's function was more that of a trading post and embarkation point, the fort itself sat on the crest of a hill along the banks of the river. Water was easily available to those within and any attackers must climb the hill that had been cleared of cover. The bulk of the very real cannons of the fort commanded the waters of the St. Lawrence River where Lake Ontario poured its waters eastward in an eternal rush to the great Atlantic.

The action at Fort Frontenac, other than the changing of the guard within the fort, was centered on the docks and on the dirt street, more of a dirt trail, that ran along the waters edge. There were trading posts and huts along the street that ran along the river and also turned up the hill away from the river. Along the hillside road were cabins and tents where the traders and Indians lived. The garrison, it was evident, slept within the fort although a few off duty soldiers could be seen walking along the docks.

Once he had decided that an attempt to capture the fort would not be feasible, Tom crawled much closer to the hillside trails with its huts. He felt that a diversion there, such as firing the huts, would probably be of less danger to his small party but still would hold the garrison to the fort.

Tomawki had found a perfect vantage point about half way up the hill and not fifty feet behind the outhouse belonging to one of the huts. He was lying between two large boulders and shielded by a heavily leafed bush. Patiently he watched the traffic on the hill for hours. Suddenly a man emerged from the hut directly in front of him and went into the outhouse to relieve himself. The figure looked familiar and Tomawki, breathing hard, waited for the man to come out. When the man finally emerged, Tom felt a surge of triumph and anticipation! It was the Frenchman, Pierre!

From that moment on one of the Onondagas kept watch on Pierre's hut. Man being a creature of habit, the watchers soon learned that Pierre went every evening at dusk to the outbuilding. His squaw usually went in the morning. Once that pattern became evident, Tom began to make his plans for revenge.

Late in the hot afternoon, the monthly supply barge from Montreal was towed by canoes across the last stretch of the Saint Lawrence River and tied to the quay below Port Frontenac. Depending upon the weather, there might or might not be another supply barge until spring. When the barge was finally moored, it was late for unloading. Leaving that chore until the morrow, the crew left a lone guard on the barge and the remainder headed halfway up the hill for the shabby hut that served as a tavern.

Tom had watched these proceedings with great interest. As the last of the bargemen stepped into the tavern, he called his group to gather around. Picking up a three-foot piece of split pine, he covered it with a thick coating of pitch that he had gathered earlier.

Handing the unlighted torch to Ahnemose, he said, "Take three warriors and go down near the river. Get reasonably close, but not too close, to the supply barge. Build a small fire as if you might be cooking a rabbit. No one will pay any attention to three more Indians in the area. Use only clean dry wood so the smoke will be minimal and not too much of an attraction for curious eyes. After a while you should be able to hear a disturbance on the hill that will draw everyone's attention, including the guards in the Fort and on the barge. When you hear the disturbance, light the torch, go up the riverbank to the barge and set it on fire. Another diversion on the hill will give you ample time to escape. When all have completed their jobs, scatter and run. We will assemble under the large tree where we spent our last night on the way here."

Ahnemose, pine torch in hand, nodded and left. Three warriors, all armed with bows followed him. Ahnemose led the way down the hill, taking care not to be seen by any watchers.

When Ahnemose was well along on his way, Tom turned to Kanakote, "You will take the rest of our party to the path leading up the hill where the tavern and shacks are located. Have half of your men make torches that can be used to fire the shacks when you hear the first disturbance. The other half of your warriors will cover the torch bearers with arrows and muskets."

"Muskets," asked Kanakote?

"Yes," replied Tom. "At that point make all the noise you can. All of you can easily fade into the forest from where you are. We must draw all eyes that way or Ahnemose could be trapped in the open banks of the lake or river."

"Will we recognize the first disturbance," asked Kanakote?

It was a chilling smile that Tom directed to Kakakote when he answered, "I think so but, at worst, you will hear me starting to give war whoops."

When all of the warriors had disappeared into the brush heading for their objectives, Tom crawled carefully, to a point directly behind Pierre's 'necessity' out building. There he hunkered down on his heels, leaning back on an oak tree that grew behind the building and shaded the area. Patiently he waited there for Pierre to come out to the building, as was his custom.

While scouting the area on previous visits, Tom had severed a two-inch thick branch that grew near the bottom of the trunk of the oak tree. He had left a full yard of the branch sticking out from the bole. The stub end was high enough off the ground to touch him in the lower abdomen when he leaned against it. On previous days he had whittled that stub end to a sharp point. When he was satisfied with the sharpness, he carefully had picked up every chip and shaving. He then had rubbed the sharpened end with dirt so that any casual glance in that direction, unlikely though it might be, would not reveal the whiteness of fresh carved wood.

It was not a long wait before Tom heard the door of the cabin open and then slam shut. Quietly he moved close to the rear wall of the "necessary" where he could hear Pierre's footsteps approaching the front of the building, the creak of the door as it opened, and the subsequent closing. Waiting for a few seconds after Pierre had entered, Tom reached around the back corner of the building and scratched the side of the building with a long stick. There was silence within as Pierre had evidently stopped to listen. Tom scratched the wall again until he heard muttered words followed by the sound of the door opening.

When Pierre stepped around the corner to the side of the building where the scratching noise had occurred, Tom moved quickly around the corner to the other side, and then around to the front of the building, passing the open door. When Tom turned that corner, he came up directly behind Pierre, who was peeking carefully around the back corner that Tom had vacated but a moment before. Before Pierre was aware of Tom's presence, that vengeful savage had grasped him by the arms just above the elbows. At a dead run, Tom ran Pierre across the small clearing and with a fierce shove he impaled him on the sharp oak so forcibly that the sharpened point of the tree limb protruded out of Pierre's back. As he clutched the body of the tree in a frantic effort to lift himself away, Pierre's screams reverberated over the fort, the river, and far out into the lake, until Tom finally brought merciful silence with his hatchet.

With Pierre's first horrible scream the guards on the parapet of the fort all came running to the landside of the fort. There they stood gazing out into the forest as the noise continued until it was suddenly cut short!

During the horrible noise, Ahnemose and his team walked down along the river to the spot where the barge guard had come out on the dock. Ahnemose was carrying the torch. The guard was looking up the hill for the source of the screams. Totally surprised, the guard fell to the ground as the arrows of the raiders thudded into his body. Without breaking stride, Ahnemose pitched his torch into the barge, which caught fire and began to burn fiercely. Ahnemose's warriors had already chopped the tie ropes. They kicked the barge so that it drifted, now burning fiercely, out into the river current. It was not very long before the powder kegs aboard the barge exploded, blowing the barge and it's contents into oblivion!

Ahnemose and his men, successful in their task, moved quickly along the side of the fort facing the river and then, climbing up, they followed close to the wall of the fort on the lakeside. When the barge exploded, they waited only a few seconds before they left the wall and ran for the woods. One French soldier, the last to leave the area of the loud screams, caught a glimpse of their flight. He fired a shot at the fleeing warriors and by great ill fortune hit the last man in the head and killed him. Ahnemose turned and fired his musket at the fort and scattered firing broke out all around.

Suddenly, every house on the trail leading up from the river burst into flames, almost at the same time. Kakanote's men had thrown their torches onto the thatched roofs. Their assignment fulfilled, they ran into the forest.

The raiders met at the designated meeting place. They had lost only one man. Tom led them through the woods. The darkness was relieved by a half moon breaking through the cloud cover and, at first, by the burning flames around Frontenac. He heard with great satisfaction the waves of intermittent, wild firing back at the fort and the blasts that signified that gunpowder had been kept in some of the burning shacks. Frontenac, he thought, would be immobilized for months to come.

Chapter XXX

The foliage was thick on the branches and there were a few yellow leaves on the trees that fell from time to time in a dancing flutter, as a reminder that the change from summer to fall was imminent. The members of the war council had assembled first at Geneseo and had then had gone up further to the beautiful lake, Skanodario. There they sat on a hill looking out on the seemingly limitless waters of the lake. The French fort at Neahgara was a leisurely hour walk to the west of them. At the foot of the hill, a fishhook shaped finger of land extended out in the lake forming a small harbor. The water was shallow far out into the lake. Large ships would run aground long before they could perceive there was a harbor there, but canoes could easily pass in and out. Sonosowah was speaking.

"As you know," he said, "Cahiague is no more. The Mohawks leveled the village to bare ground. In a year the brush and saplings will take over and no trace will remain. The men were slain and the women and children have been divided so as to be adopted by our various nations."

Raising his hand, he pointed west across the end of the lake and continued, "Now it is the turn of the rest of the Huron snakes. Aragaritka is next!"

A rumble of approval ran through the listeners. Amidst the humming murmurs of conversation, one of the pine chiefs rose and asked, "Will the attack be early in the spring?"

Sonosowah nodded and replied, "We shall gather our supplies here and ship them at night to the far shore of the lake. From there we will carry them inland."

The Pine Chief frowned and threw his hands out, palm up, in a gesture of questioning bewilderment, saying, "The streams will be flooded and the ground marshy. Our warriors carrying supplies will be weary and cold from the journey. I like it not! This could be a death trap!"

Tomawki rose to his feet with a wolfish grin and answered the Chief, "The supplies go now, not in the spring, to a cache not distant from the Aragaritka villages."

Pausing for effect, he continued, "And not only the supplies but the major force of our warriors. We shall spend the winter close by their villages."

The Pine Chief, stunned by the concept of those words, slowly sank to his seat.

Fort Neahgara was kept under siege. Although there were no attacks on the fort, no member of the garrison who placed value on his hair would venture more than a few steps from the range of the guardian guns on the walls of the fort. The crops, squash and corn, were harvested under the watchful eyes of the gunners who stood by their loaded cannons with burning port fires in their hands. No hour went by that the watchers in the fort did not see painted Senecas slipping along the tree margins just out of gun range. Tension was in the air and around the clock vigilance was the order in the fort.

Meanwhile, not far to the east in the shallow harbor there was great activity. Night after night, after darkness had fallen so movement was unseen by the watchers on the walls of the fort, huge freight canoes loaded with supplies were being paddled. They traversed across the lake, beyond the current of the river, to the western end of Lake Skanodario, also known as Ontario. Once on that side, the contents were removed from the canoes and moved to a stockpile cache three days to the northwest. Then the canoes returned, also traveling by night.

At the east end of the lake, the Mohawks and Oneidas kept a constant movement of war parties in force, which served to make communication between Montreal and Frontenac almost impossible. Communication between Montreal and the western outposts of Michimillemackinac and Dutroit was also almost impossible. Messengers and supplies were forced to take the long, arduous trip up the Ottawa and across Nipissing as a result.

As autumn crept on, it had become common to find a film of ice on the water in the buckets when one arose in the morning. At last one of the messages, carried in that necessarily roundabout route, arrived for Saint Jean in the Huron village where he was staying. In the letter from the Commandant at Fort Frontenac was a description of the terrible death of Pierre, and how it seemed apparent that his death had been carefully orchestrated. Saint Jean was much affected by the letter and for several days thereafter he sat and pondered over the events of the past year.

Aloud, he wondered, "Where could Francois Vizena be? Why have I not heard from him or, at least, heard something about him? One would have to suppose he was dead! Did those Iroquois who pursued us across the mountains into the Ohio country kill him? Who was the huge Indian who led that pursuit? A man that massive should be known outside the confines of the Iroquois tribes. Could it have been he who threw the hatchet at me at the Onondagas fight?"

He walked out of his hut and sat on a stone where he drew aimless diagrams in the dust at his feet while he continued his thoughts.

"Was it a fluke that Pierre met such a horrible and painful death, or could it be, as the commandant had indicated, a deliberate act? If deliberate, then why? What could Pierre have done, that I would not have known about, that might have singled him out for such an evil and terrible revenge?"

For a long while Saint Jean reflected on the past as he looked out over the water while he chewed on the end of the stick and tried to make sense of things. A vagrant idea began to work its way into his thoughts.

"The big warrior who threw the axe at me when we retreated from the Onondagas battle - did he spike the gun? Could he have been the one who chased us up through the Ohio country?"

Closing his eyes, St Jean slumped down and tried to reconstruct the rapidly moving events that occurred in the flight from the Onondagas battle. Sitting up suddenly, his eyes opened wide and said aloud, almost shouting, "Without loosing his grip on his hatchet he could have reached out easily and killed that French soldier who ran directly past him. But he did not! Instead, he looked directly at me and threw specifically at me. He knew me! He wasn't interested in anyone else! He meant to kill me. Why? Why!"

Thoroughly disconcerted, Saint Jean rose to his feet. Still speaking aloud, he cried, "I cannot stand the thought of a winter alone in a Huron village with nary a touch of civilization. Montreal may be out of the question, but Pontchartain is not too many days away, and French is spoken there!"

In the morning he was gone. His departure may well have sealed the fate of the Huron Wyandots. Had he stayed, Saint Jean's suspicious mind might have smelled the trap.

Chapter XXXI

The supply cache was set up at a distance far enough away from the Huron villages that casual hunting parties would be unlikely to stumble on it. From the standpoint of the Hodenosaunee, it was only a one-day forced march of fifty miles. The freight canoes continued to ply back and forth at night for several weeks until the cache held enough to support a large force, almost indefinitely. The task had strained the resources of all of the Five Nations, but at last it was completed. Tom and some two hundred warriors of the Western nations, Seneca, Cayuga, and Onondagas built log cabins to house them. Then the warriors settled in to live off the land around them throughout the fierce winter months that, even now, were upon them. The winter, bitter cold that it was, was ideal for their purpose. The snow was deep enough that the Hurons did not stray far from their villages close to the great lake named for them. Despite the winter, game was plentiful. For most of the time there was fresh red meat to go with the charred corn from the cache, corn being the diet staple for Tomawki and his men. Periodically, scouts on snowshoes would check on the Huron villages from a discrete distance.

Early March brought a few days of mild weather and Tom sent out scouts to watch for any Hurons. The scouts were recalled when the wintry weather set in again, but with the coming spring the camp bustled in preparation for the sustained good weather that would soon arrive. About the fourth day after the mild spell, the force was augmented by the arrival of nearly a thousand more warriors. The reason for the vast stockpiles of food that had been stored there in the fall was now apparent to all.

John G. McConahy

The scouts, who had so carefully watched the Huron villages, briefed the newcomers as to the contour of the land, water, position of the villages, and what other factors they might find. Tom spoke time and time again to small groups to emphasize the need for subtlety and teamwork when the moment of battle arrived.

To the group of Oneidas that Shikellamy had led into camp, Tom gave the most important and difficult task. While the rest of the warriors attacked the first of the Huron villages, Shikellamy and his force were to position themselves between that village and those farther up the lake so that no one could escape to warn the other Huron towns. That is unless and until it was desirous for some Hurons to seem to "escape". The Oneidas were not to engage in the attack at all, unless Shikellamy received specific orders from Tom. For a time, Tom thought that even his loyal friend, Shikellamy might revolt against such restrictions for they, like everyone else, were spoiling for a fight. The Oneida's anger at this non-combative role was eased when he learned what Tomawki's plan was for the other villages. It was then he realized the faith his leader had in his ability to carry out such a tricky maneuver!

The waiting hours seemed interminable. Time and time again the weapons were sharpened and oiled until at last the fateful day arrived. In the darkness, Tomawki led the warriors following the trail. They were directed by the guides who had gone out the day before and were now positioned every half-mile along the way. The party was thus able to move at a rapid pace despite the blackness of the night, relieved only by a smattering of pale moonlight from a quarter moon in a cloudy sky. The attacking force was in position surrounding the Huron town before dawn and Shickellamy had his warriors extended in a line on the north side of the village to intercept those who escaped from the village. They were there to insure that there would be no warning for the other Huron villages until the Hodenosaunee were ready.

The tricky portion of Shikellamy's assignment and one of special importance involved an angular gully that followed along with a rise that looked down on the village. The gully was almost invisible from a side view at a distance not too many feet away. This gully was a natural "unseen" escape route and Tomawki had carefully explained to the Oneidas that he wanted to be sure the gully was used by some of the survivors. However, none were to be allowed to escape until they had seen the activity that he wanted them to report. It was a difficult task for Shikellamy and his men to unobtrusively shunt some of the fleeing Huron into the gully, hold them there "undiscovered" until they had clearly seen the drama that would be unfolded on the "stage" below. Finally they were to permit those survivors to slip away in an apparently natural escape, after they had been well impressed by the strength of the attacking force.

The arrival of two hundred Seneca warriors just prior to the start of the march had brought the numbers of the attacking force to some fifteen hundred warriors, now waiting there impatiently in the thin snow. Silently they followed Tomawki, swarming into the village. Suddenly their whoops and shouting roared out as they threw coals from the cooking fires that were in the compound into the huts. The sleeping Hurons awoke and staggered out of the burning buildings only to meet sudden death outside. And many there were who died within in the flames. It was a brutally efficient slaughter because of the total surprise. Mercifully, it was over quickly. Any captives, all women and children, were grouped for return with fifty of the Senecas. Those who survived the march to the Long House would be adopted into the tribes and thus add to the strength of the League.

Meanwhile warriors kept pouring down into the village in various sized groups. Whooping as they ran, they made a constant, and overwhelming show of force. When a group would charge into the smoke and flames that almost obliterated any visibility, Tom would route those men behind a covering knoll. From there they would emerge again within sight of the surviving Hurons who were "hidden" in the gully, and again charge the village. Those Huron watchers were given the impression that there were limitless thousands of attackers. When Shikellamy felt that the Hurons hiding in the gully were sufficiently impressed by the overwhelming numbers, he gave the signal for his Oneidas to charge the village and leave the way open for the survivors to slip out of the gully and escape unnoticed, or so they thought.

When the survivors arrived in the other villages of Aragaritka their stories brought terror to the hearts of the inhabitants who then had no thought of resisting the teeming multitudes of Iroquois. As the Iroquois would approach a village, the inhabitants would flee and scatter. Tom's men would then burn the villages and the food caches. Village after village fell in such a fashion so that the whole of the Huron coast was devoid of its previous inhabitants. Aragaritka was finished. The Huron Nation as an entity was destroyed with practically no loss of life for the attacking forces. A large number of the scattered Huron were later assimilated into the tribes of the Five Nations. The rest scattered to the North and to the West.

Tom had hoped to find Saint Jean among the Huron but was disappointed to learn from a captured French half-breed that Saint Jean had gone on to Fort Pontchartain duTroit. Tom could only shake his head and wonder at the elusiveness of the Frenchman.

Chapter XXXI

Atsego was discouraged. When he and his Tuscarora companions had first arrived in Philadelphia, they had gone directly to the Governor's Mansion to seek Brother Onas and deliver the eight belts of white wampum that Nachininga had entrusted to him. To their dismay, they found that Brother Onas was in England and evidently in disgrace. The man who had replaced William Penn, Governor Evans, flatly refused to see Atsego and his group. Day after day, they were shuttled from one person to another and were given short shrift from all those they did see. Finally, Atsego sent the Tuscaroras back to Nachininga. Since they spoke no English, he feared for their safety, and he wanted the Tuscarora chief to know that he would persist. Now he leaned, glumly, against a tree and stared vacantly at the tavern across the Broad Street. He could visualize the Captain and the Doctor in that place many years before.

Suddenly, on an impulse, he stood and walked down the street where the nice Quaker lady ran a store in her husband's absence. Seeing her at the door, he approached her and said, "Good Morning."

"Oh, Atsego," she said, "I was looking for you! Have you heard that Governor Evans has left and gone to Wyomissing to meet with the Lenape, I believe?"

"No!" answered Atsego, "but I must follow him even should he go to the Ohio."

Mrs. Kohl shook her head, because she had learned to like Atsego in their short acquaintance, and called to him as he turned away, "If you go that far, ask about my man, Jakob!"

Atsego had been plodding along, following an ill defined trail along a valley - really a steep sided ravine - until he came to a huge split rock that separated the valley into upper and lower ends. As he stepped around the stone to continue on his way, he was startled by a voice close by saying, "Truly my dream would seem to be real!"

Reaching for his knife, Atsego whirled and ducked at the same instant in self defense, but the voice continued, "Peace, warrior, I would have talk with you."

Thus did Atsego and Shikellamy meet.

The two looked each other over carefully with more than casual examination, and finally their glances locked eye to eye. Satisfied with what he saw, Atsego sheathed his knife and walked over to face the other, saying as he nodded his head in acknowledgement, "I am called Atsego."

He looked away for a moment at a distant tree-covered ridge and then more intently at the rock strewn valley and finally continued, "I am a messenger and I seek Brother Onas' deputy, the man who has gone to Wyomissing, but I felt strongly that, when I entered this valley, I had been drawn here."

Shikellamy laughed and waved Atsego to a seat on a stone beside him. "I have a story for you," he said, "and I have reason to believe that our lives are, in some way or other, woven together. I am called Shikellamy and I am a Pine Chief of the Hodenosaunee. I have been troubled for some time now because of the disappearance of a friend so I fasted for seven days to cleanse my thoughts, and hopefully, to prepare me for a revelation. On the seventh night of my fast I had a dream. In this dream the great Hiawatha appeared and spoke to me. He directed me to return, once more, to the valley, this valley, where once the wolves had nearly finished me, to await a stranger who is not a stranger. Hiawatha said that man would come to me here."

Looking up, he asked Atsego, "Do you bear a message for me? I know you are a stranger, and yet I have the sensation of knowing you. I can feel the Orenda that binds us together."

Atsego leaned forward, his left elbow on his knee, his chin propped in his hand and his gaze fixed on Shikellamy's face. After a long period of thought, he replied, "Yes, we are strangers to one another. The sense of Orenda is on me also, and I feel close to you though we have never met. Yes, I bear a message, but it is not, or was not, meant for you. Now, I wonder!"

Pausing for a moment only, he continued, "I bear eight belts of white wampum from the Shaman Nachininga of the Tuscarora to Brother Onas."

Shikellamy, puzzled and frowning, said, "We are indeed strangely met for you are far above the city where Brother Onas lives."

Then there was a silence between them that stretched into minutes as both stared at the ground while they pondered the significance that might attend their meeting. Finally Shikellamy looked over at the Susquehannock and said, "Seemingly, there is a connection between us though I cannot determine what it might be. Perhaps we should start with you, as an individual. Again tell me who and what you are."

The other apologized and said, "I am Atsego, a Susquehannock. I am one of the few who remain as such in name since the Susquehannocks were defeated years ago and absorbed into the Five Nations. I have lived for many years in the Carolinas."

"With the Tuscaroras?" asked Shikellamy.

"No," answered Atsego, "though I have spent much time with them and have been accepted by them. Now I act as their messenger."

Tossing a handful of dried leaves in the air, he continued to speak, "You will, no doubt, find it odd that I have lived in the Carolinas with the pale faces. I stayed in Charlestown for many years until my friend, Doctor Woodward, died and our son was raised and sailed for England."

Shikellamy's curiosity was piqued by Atsego's words, and he asked, "You speak of a Doctor, a medicine man, and say 'our son', as if you two men were parents. What do you mean? I can tell you that the medicine man intrigues me."

Atsego was surprised by the Oneida's interest but answered quickly, "The Doctor and I were named God parents of the babe by his true father, the Captain. We were shipwrecked while sailing from Philadelphia to the Carolinas."

"Philadelphia!" interjected Shikellamy.

"Yes, Philadelphia, and both the Captain and his wife died within a day of each other. The Doctor and I were the young lad's only parents. The Doctor taught him his letters and medicine and the ways of the white man. I taught the boy the way of the wilderness, and an apt pupil was our son, Tawde."

"Tawde," shouted Shikellamy, springing to his feet, and the glade rang with the violence of his yell. Quickly, he held out his hand to calm the amazed Susquehannock. "Tawde," he repeated. "That is it! Your son is the connection. He is the man we call Tomawki!"

"Tawde," said Atsego in wonder, "You seem to know Tawde, but you couldn't. Tawde is across the water in England."

Shikellamy now was smiling and said, "Your son, Tawde, is a white man, a big man?" He continued when the other nodded, "He is as broad in the shoulder as you are and, holding his hand a foot above his own head, much taller?"

Atsego said in complete bewilderment, "Yes, he is but..."

Shikellamy interrupted, "Have you heard of the appearance of the prophesied warrior that Deganawidah predicted would come?"

Atsego answered, "That story has flown from campfire to campfire from the great ocean to the Father of the Waters and beyond. But what has this to do with us and where have you met Tawde?"

Still smiling Shikellamy said, "I am beginning to understand, although the Orenda is only partially clear to me. It is not for me to give you answers, yet you shall have them. Pick up your belts of white wampum. Forget Wyomissing, and let us hasten now to Kanatakowa, Onondaga's Castle, where there will be an assemblage and you shall have explanations. Older and wiser heads than I must talk now. I cannot tell you more."

Chapter XXXI

The trickle of fugitives rapidly swelled into a flood of humanity pouring into Pontchartain duTroit. That Aragaritka had been destroyed was, for a while, incomprehensible. The overwhelming strength of the Iroquois was difficult to believe except that eyewitness observers described the hordes in the first attack. Even discounting natural exaggeration, Saint Jean could visualize thousands of warriors.

The confidence of the French officers at the Fort and their conviction that Pontchartain was too strong and too distant was very reassuring. That is, until he talked with the Indians who traded at the Fort. Even the Plains Indians, Sioux, Pawnee, and Illinois, told stories of Iroquois war parties that had raided their territories in the past.

Deeply perturbed, Saint Jean questioned DeLery, the engineer who had designed and supervised the construction of Fort Niagara when that young man had passed through on his way to Michimillemackinac.

"No," said DeLery, "Niagara is not vulnerable. Niagara can easily withstand any attack unless it is one backed by heavy artillery and there is no such weight of cannon closer than the Atlantic coast. Furthermore, they will not be stretching their forces out so far now that we have an armed sloop on Lake Erie and Frontenac has been fully garrisoned with fresh troops."

Alphonse La Tonty, the garrison commander at duTroit, when questioned by Saint Jean, merely laughed and said, "We have scouts scattered throughout the land intervening between here and the Niagara. We would be informed and waiting long before any

Iroquois war parties could reach us. We'd have a warm welcome for them when they arrived."

Thus reassured, though ever a little skeptical, Saint Jean relaxed and enjoyed the passing of winter and the imminent advent of spring. He spent his time drinking within the fort and in his cabin, close by the wall of the fort. He frolicked with the Huron squaws from the encampment on the riverbank below the fort. Nonetheless, he was edgy and dissatisfied. As the trees greened and the spring freshets subsided, he thought about returning to Montreal. Possibly he might be able to return to France. Time had probably healed the wounds that had brought about his hasty departure. The thought of the trip the long way around through Michimillemackiac and down the Ottawa River did not sit well with him and so he tarried while he contemplated one way of return after another.

They were not exactly an imposing force. There were only six men in each of the six canoes that swept out of the Genneseo River onto the rippled waters of the lake.

"Thirty-six men," Tom murmured aloud as the thoughts raced through his mind of the counsel Sonosowah and Tehwahnears had given him before he had left.

"It is too early in the year to carry a full size war to the French and their sucklings, the Huron and Ottawa. However, they do not expect a strike from us either. If you have to, just go there, observe, and return unseen. Don't engage in any small action. However, if you can strike a hard blow that hurts and frightens our enemy, then do so. You have a minimum force, but enough for a hard strike should the opportunity present itself. Yet your group is not so large that it cannot be easily hidden from the enemy."

Gazing into glowing coals of the fire, Tehwahnears marshaled his thoughts,

Then the Seneca continued, "A good strike will cause panic at the convergence of the waters that the French call 'duTroit', and word will spread quickly. It will indeed   give pause to the Illinois, Sauk, and Miami should they even have thought of taking up the hatchet with the French."

Then Tehwahnears had looked Tom squarely in the face and spoke clearly and earnestly. "I knew in my heart it was true when Atotarho declared the prophesy of Deganawida, that you were the one! Nonetheless, be not rash, be careful and be wary. Bring back our warriors, for we may need them in the not so distant future."

The canoes moved across the mouth of the Niagara by moonlight and hugged the shore of the lake. The wind had diminished during their travel as though by angels blessed. Though the northeast wind made monstrous waves out in the lake itself, the trees of the sheltering shore permitted only a series of small dancing wavelets to form. The westerly thrust of the East wind pushed them on their way like a gentle fatherly hand.

Ahnemose, seated in the bow of the canoe in front of Tom, suddenly pointed to an almost invisible low finger of land that seemed to stretch as far as Tom could see.

"There is the 'Arrow', a long point of land that extends so far out into the lake that the wind would trouble us should we try to go around it." "

Fortunately," he continued, "there is a portage path across it. We will carry the canoes to the far side of the 'Arrow' and rest there till tomorrow."

"How far," asked Tom, "to the landing place beyond?"

"Pelee," answered the Seneca, "is a point more like the head of the arrow rather than the shaft like this one. Pelee will be two or three days paddling, depending on the mood of the wind and water."

High winds and rain held the party on the Long Point the next day. The savage reaction of the lake with a hard west wind amazed Tom.

"How quickly the lake changes and how quickly gentle ripples can become huge crashing waves. Truly the ocean itself is not so changeable."

The warriors all nodded agreement.

The guide, Kakonote, replied, "I have traveled with war parties to Michemillemackinac, and beyond. Of all the five great lakes this is the most changeable. When the Manitou of the lake so desires then will we travel and not until then."

The wild weather subsided overnight and on the eve of the third day the party landed on the point called Pelee. There they filled their canoes with stones and sank them in a small sheltered bay. From there they began their travel over land. Slowly and carefully they travelled across the broad peninsula that stuck out like a thumb to the west from the main body of land. The peninsula pointed at the narrow waters between the river called duTroit and the lake. On their ninth day of travel, Kakanote called Tom to the edge of a bluff and pointed across the narrow isthmus at Fort Pontchartain duTroit. The raiders had arrived at their destination!

Chapter XXXII

It is a recognized fact that, throughout the ages, petty jealousies in high places have, time and time again, altered the ultimate course of history. Not the least of those instances would have been the bickering in the French Court at Versailles that brought about the dismissal of Antoine de la Mathe Cadillac as the French Governor General of the Northwest Territories. Cadillac knew the territory well. Not long after he left France he had spent days in complete seclusion in Quebec City with LaSalle's veteran lieutenant, the experienced, one-handed Henri de Tonty. Deliberately, Cadillac slowly traveled westward to his command along the trade route, the protected lifeline to the west. Their passage led up the Ottawa River, across Lake Nipissing, down the French River and out onto the great open bay, later to be called by the English the Georgian Bay. They paddled across the upper region of the bay for a few hours and then turned north into the opening of Mahzenazing, a narrow high walled canyon-like waterway that ran due west for mile after protected mile. At last they came out on the open waters of the lake of the Hurons. Over the open waters they traveled past Manitoulin until at last they reached their destination, the trading post at Michimillemackinac. There, Cadillac set up his command post.

In the next few months Cadillac established a solidly garrisoned fort at Mackinac and then busily traveled over his fief to examine strategic points and make sure the trade route was protected. One of his first decisions was to build a fort on the strategic narrow straits, du Troit, which connected the upper and lower great lakes. This he named Fort Pontchartain duTroit after his mentor, the Minister of France. The Fort soon became known simply as duTroit or Detroit. Not long after this, Pontchartaine fell out of favor at court. Subsequently, Cadillac was removed from his office and ordered to Louisiana, a move that was to cost the French colonial ambitions dearly.

Tom lay in his place of concealment on the south bank and gazed across the river at Fort Ponchartain duTroit. What he saw was a well-built fortification situated in a commanding position on a high steep bank that overlooked the strait. From his vantage point, Tom noted a large creek that flowed from the left or west side of the fort. The creek had cut a deep gully that guarded the side of the fort much as a moat guards a castle. The right or east side was a large flat, cleared area of dried grass that extended around to include the north side of the fort as well. Any attacking force would have to move across the open area with no concealing cover.

The fort itself was a log palisade that enclosed a good-sized area. There was a watch turret on each corner and two entrance gates on the long east side. Later he would learn there was another gate on the north side as well as two "slip out" gates on the other two sides. Several lackadaisical sentries guarded the two main gates that were visible to Tom. They seemed to spend most of their time lazily leaning against the outer wall of the stockade. Seldom did any one of them give more than a desultory glance at the colorful, constant stream of trappers, soldiers, Indians, priests and traders that paraded in and out of the fort.

At the foot of the bluff where the fort was situated there was an encampment of several hundred Hurons on the flat area along the riverbank. Tom guessed they were probably fugitives from Aragaritka. On his side of the river directly below his vantage point was an Ottawa village of nearly a thousand people. Pulled up on the banks of both sides of the river were many canoes that made transportation back and forth quite easy. Some of the canoes were equipped with small masts and sails. Apparently most of the canoes were for the common use.

Under Tom's watchful gaze, Ahnemose, clad in ordinary leather leggings and jacket, carrying only his knife in his belt, stepped out of concealment in the woods. Slowly, completely unhurried, he walked down the hill toward the village. As he moved he stopped from time to time, seeming to examine something along the way. When he reached the tents, he could see that no one in the outskirts had spared him the slightest glance. Without hesitation he casually strolled through the Ottawa village as if he belonged there. When Ahnemose reached the river, he walked down the bank and disappeared from view. Shortly afterward, he reappeared paddling a canoe toward the far bank. He was towing three empty canoes behind him. Others from the village had been observed doing the same thing to even the distribution on the two sides.

As Ahnemose neared mid-stream he gradually slowed his pace and unobtrusively slipped out of sight downstream around the bend of the river. Such actions were apparently commonplace since no one in the village seemed to notice. Shortly thereafter Kakanote did the same. In a very short period of time the group had gathered enough canoes in a little secluded backwater below the Ottawa village for them all to cross. They crossed that night under cover of darkness.

Once they had arrived in a backwater lagoon on the far shore, they filled their canoes with stones. There they would be readily available, if they were suddenly needed. Having taken care of their canoes, the group worked around the fort in a wide circle. Finally they took up a position that was hidden in a small copse of trees looking out over a grassy field. Their place of cover was about two hundred paces from the east side of the fort. Through the remainder of the day they lay concealed in the copse and watched the fairly continuous traffic that went in and out of the eastern gates.

They observed that there were a number of small nondescript groups of Indians that sat around in various areas of the grassy field. The groups, as far as they could see, were from a number of different tribes. Most, but not all, seemed to be waiting there for companions who were in the fort. On the following day, Tom, Ahnemose, Kakanote, and Shikellamy sat openly in the sunlight in front of the trees. They attracted no attention.

Tom leaned back against a tree and spoke to the others. "While we are sitting here waiting to determine how we can best hurt our enemies, let us consider ways and means of escape from here, when the time comes. It would be wise to have several possibilities."

Not wishing to be so obvious as to point, Tom nodded his head toward the strait on his left and said, "Starting with the canoes, it is obvious that we must delay pursuit by destroying those we leave behind. Just make sure that we have one of those sail canoes available. If any of our party should be injured and unable to travel, I will take them in the sail canoe down the river and out into the lake.

With good fortune we have a chance to catch a west wind that could carry us to Tanawundaga or with a north wind to the Ohio lands."

Kakanote said, "We could all go that way if we have to."

The others nodded their heads solemnly in agreement, but Ahnemose quickly said, "The little river would be better, I think."

Tom nodded agreement. Then he leaned forward and drew in the dust with his finger.

"This," he said, "is the large river that we saw entering the strait just below the lagoon where we launched the canoes. I think that stream has to be the one we crossed some fifteen miles inland when we came overland from Pelee Point. Keep that in mind for a quick retreat. We can take the canoes right upstream. There's plenty of water.

Raising his eyes from the river, Tom looked thoughtfully at five somewhat ramshackle, thatch roofed cabins that had been built only a few feet away from the wall of the fort.

"The careful man who built this fort', he mused, "would never have permitted those buildings. They would make a very nice fire and probably would damage the fort as well."

The others were in agreement. Tom leaned over to Ahnemose and said, "Brother you have been out here for several hours before we came out. What of interest have you seen?"

Ahnemose smiled and answered, "I was going to call you out before this but I wanted to be sure." Ahnemose's eyes opened wide as he continued, " I have seen the Frenchman, the one you seek, Tomawki, and he lives in the fourth hut from the gate. You can kill him tonight!"

"Softly, my friend", said Tom. "I was not sent here to lose warriors for the sake of killing one man. He deserves killing it is true, but perhaps not this time. Sonosowah and Tewahnears sent us here to make a lasting impression on the French and to teach them all a lesson. Saint Jean will die soon enough, but first, the lesson."

"Kakanote", Tom said, "Take a couple of warriors with you to cover you although I don't think anyone will pay attention to a couple more Indians. See if it is feasible to move one of those sail canoes down below to our assembly place. It might be best to do so after dark."

After Kakanote departed Tom continued his observations. "With our small force, fire would be our best weapon. Those shacks and the grass on this plain will burn like tinder once they are lit. As close as those buildings are to the fort even they should catch fire. The fires and other unplanned occurrences might make it difficult for our people to assemble for our escape."

Right at that moment a hiss from the wooded area demanded their attention. There was Kakanote, already returned, waving for them to come back into the woods. When he stepped behind the veil of trees, Tom saw, to his astonishment, a bound and gagged Indian sitting in the midst of his men. The stranger had a narrow scalp lock of long finger length hairs. They had been treated with something that made them stand straight out despite their length. The man wore common leather clothing and the skin of his face and arms were smeared with dirt so that no shining skin could be seen.

Kakanote grinned and told Tom, "I wouldn't have seen him under his pile of brush and leaves if he hadn't moved."

Then Kakanote shook his head and went on, "He didn't know we were there or I guess he would have laid still. We were coming back from looking down at the canoes and were sneaking along quietly. We didn't want anyone in the woods to know we were around. When we saw him, we jumped him before he could see us and give us away. We didn't kill him because we could see he was spying on the fort. I thought you might want to see him."

Tom looked speculatively at the stranger. The man's mouth was working behind the gag as if he wanted to talk. After a moment of thought Tom said, "Can you understand me?"

When the man nodded his head, Tom said to his men, "Ungag him but if he opens his mouth to call out, kill him!

Do you understand that", he said to the stranger." Again the man nodded.

Ahnemose aimed an arrow at the stranger's heart and said, "If you raise your voice, you are dead!"

The strange Indian, when his mouth was free, asked, "Who are you?"

Ahnemose answered, "More to the point, who are you and what is your tribe?"

"I am Sanatan of the Sauk Nation, and you, I know, are not of the Ottawa, Huron, or Algonkin!"

Ahnemose answered proudly, "We are the Hodenosaunee. We are those whom the French call the Irakwai!"

The eyes of the Sauk widened perceptibly as he murmured, "Irakwai"? He looked then at Ahnemose and imperiously waved aside the arrow pointed at his heart.

"What do you here", he asked? "You are no friends of those over there", he said, motioning his hand toward the fort. Then the Sauk looked around the group and continued, "There is a story that has been passed around the fires that the Irakwai have a new leader who has come to lead in war. Is this true?"

Ahnemose quietly answered, "Only the Hodenosaunee call it Osquesont. Other tribes have another name."

Pointing across the circle at Tom he said, "Behold! There stands Tomawki, the Battle Leader of the Hodenosaunee!"

Now the eyes of the Sauk turned toward Tom and they widened in surprise. "A white man is the Battle Leader! It is true then that you must be here to hurt the French. The French are no friends of the Sauk, and we watch them carefully. If we can help you, we will!"

Tom smiled and replied, "The Sauk are well known for their bravery and their hatred of the French. We will forge a solid bond for the future with our friends, the Sauk. I have an idea that will hurt the French. I think we can have great success and still get away from here unscathed. How many men are with you? Six, you say? This is how we will do it."

Chapter XXXIII

Tom was inside the cabin, leaning against the wall on the hinged side of the door, where he would be concealed when the door opened. The door was slightly ajar, as he had left it. Light from the wick in a hollow stone oil lamp dispelled the absolute darkness but its position in a corner caused its glow to bathe the room in dull grimy grayness. Tom was trying to control his breathing by forcing himself to take deep breaths with measured slowness. His hands were wet with perspiration from the excitement of the moment.

Cold rage stormed within him as his thoughts went back to Oneonta, lying in her grave beside the rippling brook. He glanced across the room to the sturdy wooden table he had pushed against the opposite wall. Lying on its back up on the table was a wooden chair braced against the wall. The legs stuck out over the table.

The crunch of gravel under a boot told Tom that the Frenchman was at hand. An angry exclamation, "Ce va!" came from Saint Jean when he saw his cabin door was open and that a light within was lit. Saint Jean stomped into the room and stopped in complete astonishment! His straw tick had been torn apart and was piled against the wall and there was broken furniture piled up on that. He had no time to wonder about the mess. When the door slammed shut behind him, he spun around, reaching for the knife at his belt. The hands that grasped his wrists were powerful under normal circumstances, but now they were enhanced by maddened rage. Saint Jean was unable to move.

The Frenchman, unused to being manhandled so easily, attempted to drop to the floor. Tom kneed Saint Jean in the groin, a move that brought a gasp of pain from the ashen face of the man.

John G. McConahy

Saint Jean looked up with agonized eyes at his painted assailant wearing a scalp lock and choked out a surprised, "A white man!"

There was no comfort in the answer, "I am Tomawki".

Saint Jean set his feet a little firmer and said, "Tomawki, the prophesied one. Your name has flown across the earth. Have mercy!"

"Have mercy", said Tom with a gentle smile that brought terror to Saint Jean's heart. "You left me to the tender mercy of Francois and the Algonkins. I killed them all and then chased you across the mountains to shores of the lake. The woman you left there with Francois became my squaw and I loved her dearly. When you led the attack at Kanatakowa, a splinter knocked loose by your cannon pierced her heart. I thought it was only fitting when I impaled Pierre on a sharpened tree limb at Frontenac not too long ago. I missed you again when I led the battle that destroyed Aragaritka, and your Hurons. Now I am here for you and, after you, the fort.

Saint Jean feigned distress and again cried, "Mercy". At the same time he attempted to twist away but the hands held him in place as if he were a child. The smile on Tomawki's face became contorted with rage. Suddenly he let go of St. Jean's wrists and heaved the Frenchman up in the air, holding him by the waist. Saint Jean rained blows on Tom's head, but to no avail. Holding his captive firmly, Tom ran across the room and slammed the Frenchman into the legs of a chair firmly braced against the cabin wall. Earlier those chair legs had been carefully whittled into needle sharp points.

Saint Jean's breath whistled from his throat. When Tom stepped back, Saint Jean fell face down on the floor. Gathering himself, he began to crawl blindly on his elbows and knees across the room. The chair, like an obscene saddle, stuck up from his back and a trickle of blood from his mouth made a trail on the floor. Halfway to the door he collapsed and a death rattle gurgled in his throat.

Tom felt his rage subside as he looked at the body of the man who had evaded his vengeance so long. Now all business, Tom stepped over Saint Jean and lit the slow fuse he had prepared earlier that led to a pile of straw and tinder against the wall. Carrying the Frenchman's pistol, he stepped out of the door and into the darkness.

Sliding along the wall of the fort, Tom reached the front corner that overlooked the cooking fires on the banks of the river below. Time was running short when he took from his belt the specially prepared hatchet with "Kanatakowa" burned on the handle. Rapping on the wall of the fort with measured taps, he waited until two French soldiers with a lighted torch leaned out of the gun ports on the corner turret. The hatchet Tom threw took one of the men full in the face. Shifting the pistol to his right hand, he shot the second man neatly in the forehead.

The roar of the pistol reverberated throughout the valley and across the grassy flats and was followed by Tom's loud war whoops. The signal thus given, fire arrows arched through the air, landing in the fort and also on the tents below. Almost at the same instant, Saint Jean's cabin burst into flames that quickly spread to the adjacent cabins.

Coincidentally, the Sauks set fire to the dry grasses that were on the northern fields on both sides of the river. Tom's warriors lit the fields on the east and south sides. The Sauks whooped loudly for a relatively short time and left.

At this juncture, pandemonium could be the only description of the scene. Some Hurons tried to flee across the river but their canoes sank from the hatchet holes Kakanote had made earlier. Some tried to flee to the Fort for protection but as Tom screamed "Iroquois! Iroquois!" and continued speaking in French, the soldiers promptly fired on the Hurons, thinking they were the attackers. Tom ran down toward the river, still shouting "Iroquois!" and scooped up several burning brands from one of the campfires. As he ran through camp, he would pause briefly to light any burnable tent or cabin. Ahnemose did the same on the Ottawa side and soon a major conflagration was roaring on both sides of the river.

Then the attackers worked their way through the mobs toward the assembly point where their canoes were concealed. Shikellamy and three of the Senecas had gone there immediately after letting loose the fire arrows and had the canoes emptied of the stones and ready to go. Tom was the last to arrive, and as he ran down the bank to the assembled group his foot slid on a wet stone. His weight came down heavily on his ankle. He suppressed a moan and tried to put his weight on his foot. The agony of the pain nearly brought out a yell.

Shikellamy, his face wrought with concern ran up to him and said "Tomawki, your ankle?"

Tom replied, "Do we have anyone dead or injured?"

"No!" answered Shikellamy, and when Tom asked about the sail canoe, Shikellamy said, "It is there."

John G. McConahy

Tom placed a hand on Shikellamy's arm and said, "I can not travel by foot. Put me in the sail canoe and push me into the channel. You, Shikellamy, take our warriors safely home. I will sail down the river into the lake. Should the winds in my Orenda favor me, I could even meet you at Pelee, but do not wait for me and worry not. I will make it somewhere, somehow. Now shove me off!"

The quarter moon came clear of its cloudy curtains and lighted his way. Two hours before dawn he came into the waters of the lake. A mild westerly wind arose and gently filled the tiny sail and set him on an easterly course. It wafted him slowly past the French sloop that plied its trade between Niagara and Dutroit

"Qui vive," came a voice from the sloop. " Who goes there and what is the glow in the night."

Digging in with a paddle to help the sail speed his progress beyond the range of the ship's cannons, Tom and the canoe melted into the darkness of the misty lake. But his voice in broken French floated back. "All is lost. English take Fort! Fly for life!" Then his voice drifted off in a smattering of nonsensical Indian language.

Though the arrival of dawn gave him light to see, the misty fog allowed him no more than one hundred yards of visibility in any direction. The lake was reasonably calm and a light wind filled the sail and pushed him steadily, he hoped eastward, leaving bedlam behind.

Meanwhile, Shikellamy led the rest of the raiding party in their canoes across the Strait, and up the river for their planned escape. Paddling furiously, they made excellent time. Some twenty miles upstream they beached their canoes on the south bank. That afternoon, on a forced march, they reached Point Pelee.

Kakonote asked Shikellamy, "Shall we wait here for Tomawki?"

Shikellamy answered, "No. Quickly into our canoes and head for Nundawaonoga. Tomawki, the Prophesied one, has an Orenda foreordained in the wampum woven by the Great Spirit. We know he will continue on to the ultimate bead of the wampum. We are not as certain of our own lives, so let us make haste for the shelter of the Long House. Let us not tempt the good luck we have had. Get into the canoes and away. Even now, the wind blows us firmly toward home. Once there we will worry about Tomawki."

Chapter XXXIV

Chillecothe, Opessah's Shawnee village, was alive with dancing dust devils as the inhabitants scurried back and forth across the central clearing. The clearing had row after row of huts and, mostly on the periphery, animal hide tents. Each person's moccasins would throw up little clouds of dust that the vagrant winds would spin into miniature tornados. The attention of most of the inhabitants was focussed on the moving figures that centered on the post in the midst of the clearing.

There, with hands tied behind her back, was the half naked figure of a woman. One end of an eight-foot rope was tied to one of her wrists, the other end to the post. Other than the limited area of the rope length, she had no way to dodge the pinches and the digs with sharp sticks that every passing squaw inflicted upon her. They all carried bundles of wood that they stacked around near her feet. Obviously they looked forward to the burning torture to come with the morning. Blonde, bewildered, and bedraggled, the woman, though beaten, was still defiant.

Meanwhile, weeks earlier Tom, fleeing from the attack on Pontchartain, had taken advantage of a brisk northwest wind to head his sail canoe directly south. He hoped to reach the nearest shore of the Ohio Country long before organized pursuit could develop. He was able to beach his canoe on a sandy strand as the sun was setting. Clearing the canoe of the useful items he had found in it, hide blankets, pemmican, and weapons, he threw together a temporary pack and limped into the forest.

Over the next few weeks he worked south away from the lake while his ankle recovered from the mild sprain. There was a vague

John G. McConahy

notion in the back of his mind that he might be able to eventually reach Charlestown. At last he stopped and made a semi-permanent camp until he determined what course he should take. He was in no particular hurry. Scouting the country around his camp, he found his only neighbors lived in the Shawnee town of Chillicothe at least ten miles away.

Even though Opessah's village was miles from his camp, Tomawki had made it a regular custom to check on the activities of his nearest neighbor in the Ohio Country. Tom usually paddled his canoe down river from time to time to visit the village. Just above Chillicothe he had discovered a slow, narrow, and deep little stream that was shrouded with heavy brush and alders. First he made his way several hundred yards up the narrow waterway where he came to a wide deep pool. The stream cascaded into the pool from above as a thirty-foot waterfall that splashed mightily and loudly into the pool from a ridge of rock. As he paddled toward the cascade a sudden gust of wind that nearly tipped the canoe, blew the curtain of water aside for a flashing moment and Tomawki glimpsed a depth behind the curtain of the falls. Then the watery shroud closed again. A quick dive under the cataract revealed the cave, a crevice behind the falls that angled back under the ridge. He was able to drive his canoe through the cascade of water. Behind it there was room enough to tie the canoe to an outcropping of rock and remain completely hidden. Once he had his gear and the canoe safely concealed, he swam out and went on foot the two some miles to Opessah's village.

This was the fourth trip that Tom had made to observe the action at Opessah's village. On this particular trip Tom was lying in his favorite observation spot under a dense flowering rhododendron bush on a wooded rise that overlooked the Shawnee village. He had seen the white woman in the camp on his previous visit. Although her movements had seemed to be restricted at that time, he thought she was a renegade. Watching the scene, he realized that she had always been a prisoner, and her time of torture and death were now at hand!

Concealing any trepidation he might have felt, Tomawki rose from his place of concealment and walked slowly down the slope and into the camp where he strolled with a quiet air of confidence. His leisurely movements were so casual that no one in the village noticed him until he came to a pause in front of the woman. He stood there for a moment, hands on hips, legs spread apart, staring

Scalpel And Hatchet

at the woman. Suddenly he stepped forward and with one hand he roughly grabbed one of her breasts. With a scream of anger she spun away from him, kicking at him as she turned.

With a laugh Tom turned away from the angry woman and faced the crowd of Shawnees who had gathered behind him. Tom knew that Opessah was the Chief from his previous observations of the camp.

Haughtily, he spoke directly to the chief. "The Hodenosaunee keep careful watch over their children, the Shawnee. I am here to see that all is well with our children. I am Tomawki, the Battle Leader of the Hodenosaunee."

The crowd behind Opessah murmured when Tom spoke his name. Tom continued his speech directed to Opessah.

"I will spend this night here. Have someone show me my place of sleeping. Have this woman brought to my tent. I will use her tonight. Tomorrow she will be yours to do as you like!"

Opessah's face showed no trace of anger but he seethed within! He shadowed his emotions because several of his hunters had encountered Senecas in the region. The Senecas had asked if the hunters had seen Tomawki.

Quietly Opessah spoke, "The prophesied warrior honors our village. Pointing to a tent on the outer edge of the clearing, he said, "The warrior, Tomawki, can rest well there. There are buffalo robes, clothing, and anything else the great one desires. This woman can serve Tomawki and meet her Orenda tomorrow. If Tomawki stays with us, there are many of the women of the Shawnee who would crave the favors of such a great warrior."

Though laughter tended to bubble inside him, Tom gave no indication of his feelings. Instead he spoke soberly, "The white woman will scream with pain and terror when Tomawki plunges his spear in her. On the morrow, she will think back on her pleasures as she burns. It will make her dying more enjoyable for the squaws."

Stepping forward to the prisoner, he cut the rope at the post, threw a loop around her neck and led her, half choking toward his assigned tent. When she attempted to kick him, he yanked her forward. With her hands tied behind her back, she fell hard with her face in the dust. Laughing, Tom pulled her to her feet and flung her into the tent. By the time he had her tied down to stakes driven in the dirt floor, darkness had fallen. Her arms and legs, tied to the stakes, were widely spread.

Tom's heart was pounding with the tension that was building. Peering out through a crack in the tent opening, he could see a quiet and serious group of Shawnee warriors sitting outside and staring expectantly at the tent. The stage was set and the show had to go on.

He was excited as he gazed at the near naked body of the woman. He had been abstinent for a long time and he could feel his passion rising. At last he threw himself on her defenseless body. Her startled scream of astonishment and then pain at his brutal entrance, followed by further screaming of rage and sobbing brought grunts of approval from the listeners outside the tent.

When he had finished, Tomawki came out of the tent and adjusted his breechclout. He smoked with the group for a while and chatted quietly with Opessah. After about an hour he arose and entered the tent again, untying his breechclout as he entered. Once again there were screams from the tent, now more from anger and also because of the responsiveness of her body. When it was over, she lay there sobbing in frustration. Tom peeked out and saw the Shawnee group had left.

Suddenly to Nancy's surprise, a hand over her mouth made noise impossible and a soft voice in her ear said in English, "I'm sorry but it had to be done and it had to be real. I think we are safe now for the night for they seem to be satisfied. Sob softly but loudly enough to be heard if any are still outside. We must get out when all is quiet in the village so the barking dogs will not arouse their curiosity."

Cutting her loose from her stakes, he said "Stretch and loosen your arms and legs while I check outside."

Returning in a moment, he took his knife and slit the back of the tent. Pointing a finger at her he said, "For your life and mine, and an ugly death it would be for both of us, do exactly as I do, move quietly and make no noise".

With those words he slid through the slit in the tent and the girl, totally bewildered, crawled out after him. As Tom had predicted, a few dogs barked but not in any unusual pattern. As the village settled into sleep, the fugitives scrambled on their hands and knees into the covering forest. The moon made enough light for Tomawki to lead the way on the river trail until he was far enough along. Then he made a turn inland and left a visible trail for their pursuers who were sure to follow in the morning light. When they reached and climbed the long ridge that led to the stream above the waterfall,

Tom turned upstream and led the way a mile or so away from the falls. At last he went carelessly down the bank and into the stream. The moon was high in the sky and dawn was only a few hours away.

At midstream, he said to her, "Stand right there. I will return but it will take a good hour. Do not go move from this spot. Do not go near the bank or sit on a rock. I will return after I cover our trail. If we do not wish to be overtaken, I must leave them some false tracks to follow."

With those words he started upstream, breaking an occasional twig as he went. After many minutes had passed, he deliberately slipped climbing a rock and left a print of a hand in the mud on the bank. Finally satisfied, he turned and hurried downstream to where the girl waited in some desperation. Taking her arm, he led her downstream staying in the middle os the stream until they reached the falls.

"Can you swim", he asked.

When she nodded affirmatively, he said, "Now we jump into the pool. When we surface, we will swim under the fails. There is a hiding place behind the curtain of water".

When he reached out to her, she placed her hand in his without hesitation and they leaped together into the pool.

The girl had a moment of fright when they dropped the thirty feet from the brink of the waterfall into the pool. Her body sank deep under the water, but a strong arm grasped her and gently pulled her to the surface. Still holding her firmly, he drew her behind him as he swam under the fall and into the small pool behind the cascade where his canoe was tied. Nancy marveled at the protected area with its secluded pool and, just beyond, the narrow ledge that rampaging spring floods had carved free from under the solid stone roof.

There was barely room enough for the two of them on the narrow moss covered ledge. As they sat there shivering, she instinctively moved closer to him for warmth and accepted as natural the warm and protective arm he placed around her. Finally, the exhausted girl drew up her knees, and lay against his chest. The warmth of the man's body comforted her and, thus contented, she slept.

Tom sat quietly not wishing to move and disturb her. His arm almost involuntarily pressed her closer to him. He sat in silence and contemplated the extraordinary bravery and quick intelligence of this woman. She had been ravished, humiliated, and angry. Still, when he whispered in her ear, she understood almost immediately what he had done and why he had done it. There had been no recriminations and she had followed him immediately. Of course she could trust no one else, but that too required great courage. During their arduous flight through the forest and up the ridge there had been no faltering and no complaints although she was obviously scratched and muscle sore. There had been no holding back on the brink of the awesome waterfall. When he said, "Jump", she jumped without hesitation. A wave of tenderness for the girl swept over him. Finally, warmed by her body, he drowsed until the light of day that came through the watery curtain began to fade and a new night was imminent.

Tom woke the girl and motioned for her to stay on the ledge. Tom slipped off the ledge into the small pool without a splash and swam to the edge of the watery curtain. Only his eyes and nose were above the water level when he eased through the falls to survey the area outside the falling water. There were no signs of any Shawnee in the vicinity. Swimming back to their hiding place, he found the girl waiting quietly.

"It will be dark in a few minutes," he said, "and we will leave. You get in the canoe. I will stay in the water and guide it from there until we reach the river."

As darkness fell while the moon was still low in the sky, Tom pulled the canoe through the edge of the falls. He maneuvered the canoe across the large pool to the point where the stream branched off on its way to the river.

Now he could wade. Leading the canoe, both he and the girl crouching low, he slowly and quietly waded along the stream. A sudden noise and a moving shadow not far ahead along the stream brought them to a startled halt. He shoved the canoe noiselessly under an overhanging bush. At last there was a grunt and the shadow rambled away. Tom leaned over the girl, now lying on the bottom of the canoe, and. whispered in her ear "bear". She nodded and squeezed his arm to show him she understood.

Hidden by the brush along the bank, Tom stood where the stream entered the river, for what seemed to Nancy, an interminable time. Satisfied at last that it was clear, he clambered into the canoe with her. Tom paddled the canoe with driving strokes to the far bank of the river. Staying close to that side, trailing one paddle behind the canoe as a rudder, they drifted downstream in the darkness, unseen, past the Shawnee camp.

After some two hours of paddling along with the push of the current, Tom pulled over to the shore and helped Nancy out of the canoe. Standing on the shore and thinking aloud so that the girl could follow his thought, he said, "They will have searched today up the stream and all over that side of the river. Probably tomorrow they will cross to this side and begin to search for us, but it will still be another day before they reach this area."

He was quiet while he considered their position and finally added, "We should be completely safe tonight, but we cannot chance a fire. Our dinner will be dry pemmican and then we must sleep. We need to be well rested tonight if we are to get beyond Opessah's reach tomorrow."

Half starved, they gobbled down the remaining bits of pemmican in Tom's pouch and then huddled together in the shelter of the base of an uprooted tree. There they had some protection from the wind. Once again, the warmth of their bodies under the deerskin robe mutually comforted them. Tom turned his head and looked down at the girl beside him even as she raised her face and looked up at him. Impulsively he brushed his lips against hers. Her shy but tender response startled him. What ensued, warmth and movement with much kissing and fondling, aroused a passion in both man and woman that consummated in love making as gentle as their first had been violent.

Chapter XXXV

For several days Atsego followed Shikellamy over mountains, streams, and grassy meadows. Each time Atsego questioned, Shikellamy merely answered with a smile and a few words. "It will be explained when we get there."

When Atsego wondered just where "There" was, he would get the same smile and a shrug of the shoulders. Finally they came to tilled fields and Atsego could see ahead of them a walled town with huts and huge long houses covered with slabs of bark.

Staring around him, Atsego followed Shikellamy through the outer gates and entered the village of Kanatakowa. He was aware that he was the center of curiosity for many of the various inhabitants. Atsego's own curiosity was aroused by the spectacle of the remnants of burned buildings. His eyes also saw the newly replaced sections of the stockade wall. He knew there had been a fierce battle fought here in the not so distant past. Thinking about what he was seeing, he followed his guide around a huge rock and into a small natural amphitheater. His wandering thoughts were jolted back to the present when he found he was standing before a council meeting of the Shamans of the League.

Even as Atsego realized where he was, a Shaman rose to his feet and spoke sharply. "Shikellamy, whom do you bring before us who is important enough to interrupt this meeting!"

Shikellamy replied in a loud voice so all present could hear, "I bring you a warrior bearing a message that was not directed to us, but rather to Brother Onas.

Wait," he said, holding up his hand to quiet their impatience, "I know not his message but," and he paused for effect, "this messenger has told me that he is the father of Tomawki, the Battle Leader of the Hodenosaunee. The father of Tomawki is hearing this for the first time. His name for the Osquesont is Tawde."

Atsego was stunned by Shikellamy's revelation. He was, for the moment, oblivious to the noise and excitement as everyone in the audience rose to their feet. Out of the group stepped a slender figure who approached and spoke to the still shocked Atsego.

"I am Dahweenet, a Shaman of peace. Since your son first came to us I have waited these many moons for you, or someone like you, to appear. The dying Deganawidah foretold of the coming of one who would be a healer of men, and he is. That he would be a great warrior and leader in battle, and he is. That he would have blood on his hands, and he does. Finally, Deganawidah said he would bring peace to the lands of the Hodenosaunee and their neighbors. That he would swell the strength and numbers of the Hodenosaunee. These last we have yet to see. My Orenda tells me your message must be of great importance. What is your message to Brother Onas?"

Words tumbled from Atsego's mouth in a constant flow like water from an upturned gourd. "Tawde here? He cannot be here! He is across the ocean in England. I would be the first to know of his return. He would let me know before he came back. It is impossible!"

Dahweenet laid a quieting hand on the agitated Susquehannock's arm and said softly, "How your son comes to be here without your knowledge is a long story. Shikellamy now has our permission to tell it to you in full later. However, rest assured that white man though he may be, Thomas MacKaye is known to our people not as Tawde, but as the Osquesont, Tomawki. He is the prophesied 'Hatchet', the Battle Leader of the League."

Now indeed was Atsego overwhelmed. He sank to a seat from which he looked around at the others with wondering eyes. With a searching look he stared up at the two burly Shamans who had stepped forward to address him. Both were nodding their heads in agreement with the Peace Shaman.

"I am Sonosowah," said the first.

"And I am Tehwahnears. We are the War Leaders of the Hodenosaunee," said the second. "It is true that Tomawki is our designated Battle Leader. With our blessing he led the successful attack on Frontenac, the successful attack that destroyed the

Aragaritka, and the successful attack on duTroit. He did not return from the last battle."

With great pain in his voice Atsego questioned, "He is dead? My son is dead!"

"No," answered Dahweenet, the Peace Shaman. "He twisted his ankle in the assault on duTroit and could only hobble. He thought he would slow his warriors in their retreat and possibly cost them their lives. He took a canoe alone and sailed out into the lake. Since then we have heard nothing from him."

"I suppose it is possible that he could be dead," continued Dahweenet. "However the Prophecy is incomplete. My Orenda tells me he lives."

"And so does mine," said Atsego, "else I would not have been directed here!"

Tehwahnears addressed the assemblage of Shamans and Pine Chiefs. "Send out runners now to all of the Nations. Call out the warriors. We shall flood the Ohio Country with our warriors until we find our missing Osquesont. Tomawki is not dead so he must be there somewhere. Find him!"

Chapter XXXVI

Grayness groped its way through the black of the night and wreathed the man and woman, sleeping together at the base of the tree, in a halo of visibility. Almost awake, Tom gently tightened his arm around the warm body of the woman and with a sigh began to slip back into contented sleep. The snap of a twig nearby jolted him instantly awake, though he moved not a muscle. Finally, he moaned softly as if still asleep and rolled slightly away from the girl, one hand flopping in the general direction of his weapons. Peering through half-slitted eyelids, he could see handle of the hatchet only a few inches from his hand. Moving his hand slowly, he was tensing his muscles for explosive action, when a moccasin stepped firmly on his wrist.

Before he could react, a familiar voice said, "No weapons, Tomawki, it is Ahnemose."

With a laugh Tom swung his body up into a sitting position. The girl opened her eyes and gave a startled cry of alarm at the five strange Indians standing around them. Terrified, she turned her head toward Tom and felt a surge of relief at the huge grin that split his countenance. Satisfied that they were not in any immediate danger, she shamefacedly tried to cover her nakedness with the blanket. She watched as Tom extended his hand and the nearest man grasped it, pulling Tom to his feet then pounding him on the back in obvious happiness.

Though the words of the conversation were too rapid for her to follow, she heard Tomawki, as she knew him, use the names Shawnee and Opessah. When the stranger repeated the names with a sneering tone, she knew instinctively that these men were not a danger to them.

Tomawki said to the Indians, "We are pursued in force by Opessah, the Shawnee, whose people once lived on the Susquehanna. He moved his people from there to Chillicothe long before the last snowfall. They were going to burn the girl when I stole her from them and they must be looking close by. Even with you and your four warriors, we are still in danger though they may not have traced us yet to this spot."

All five of the newcomers burst into laughter. Speaking slowly so the bewildered girl might catch the drift, Ahnemose said, "We five are only a few of the hundreds of Hodenosaunee in the Ohio country. There are several hundred in gunshot distance. Yesterday Tehwahnears and Sonosowah, the War Leaders, spoke at some length to Opessah. The Peace Shaman, Daweenet, listened quietly to the conversation, gently shaking his head in agreement. The leaders explained to Opessah that the waters would continue to flow in the Ohio portion of Hodenosauneega whether the Shaxwee live or die, and not in some distant future, but now!"

Once he understood such a simplified picture, Opessah determined that it was getting well into the time that the spring crops should be planted. Great farmers that they are, the Shawnee hastened to return to Chillicothe to do those chores that had slipped their minds.

Laughing, Tom leaned over to the girl and told her, "The Shawnee met large groups of my people of the Five Nations. These five Senecas are a small party, but there are many more nearby. They tell me Opessah has returned to his village. We are quite safe."

Turning back to Ahnemose, he asked, "What event or disaster has brought the Hodenosaunee in such great numbers to the Ohio, especially with both of the War Shamans and one Peace Shaman, as well?"

"Very simple," answered Ahnemose. "They were looking for, or seeking word of, a missing Osquesont - you!"

"For me?" said Tomawki stepping back. His voice showed his deep concern as he continued. "Is the war enlarged? Have we been attacked again, or are we attacking? I do not understand why the Peace Shaman, Dah...?"

With a smile Ahnemose cut him off, saying, "All of the Peace Shamans sent Dahweenet as their delegate to speak to you. To make the search easier and quicker, the Oneida and Seneca came in force. The War Leaders came to direct the search and to be at hand should a fight ensue. A large force of the warriors of the other nations are positioned on the Allegheny where they are close enough to protect the Long House, yet available should they be needed here."

With a laugh Tom said, "I can well understand Opessah's reluctance to search further for us!" Then he murmured in wonder, "The whole League out looking for me. Why?"

Ahnemose stared vacantly into the distance, collecting his thoughts. "I have news of great interest for you."

Speaking in measured tones for emphasis, Ahnemose continued, "Thirty suns ago, Shikellamy, who had been missing for a short time, reappeared leading a big Susquehannock warrior. He brought the man before the Council of Shamans who were meeting at Kanatakowa. Shikellamy had earlier had a dream. In this dream Hiawatha spoke to him and directed him to go to the valley of the wolves, a place where the wolves had surrounded him when he broke his leg many moons ago."

A look of wonder crossed Tom's face. He asked, "The place where Shikellamy and I first met?"

"Exactly," answered Ahnemose. "And as it happened to the son, so it did to the father."

Hurrying his words so as to keep Tomawki from interrupting, Ahnemose went on, "The Susquehannock had been given a message and eight belts of white wampum by the Tuscarora Shaman, Nachininga, that he was to deliver into the hands of Brother Onas. Brother Onas is across the Great Water and his deputy left Philadelphia and went to Wyomissing. The messenger started towards Wyomissing, but was strangely drawn to the valley of the wolves. There he met Shikellamy. In this almost sacred valley, Shikellamy felt his Orenda strong within him, and so he took the man with his message and belts of wampum to the council of the Hodenosaunee. The father of Tomawki was heard with great deference."

Tom's voice trembled with excitement as he nearly shouted the words, "My father! You mean the Susquehannock is my father, Atsego!"

"Yes, your father, Atsego." was the answer. "You will learn more from your guides as you go, but now time is important and you must be gone. The three sachems await you impatiently a long day's trot from here."

Looking at the girl, shrouded in her blanket, he added, "You'll have to leave the woman."

"Wait," he said, as Tom opened his mouth to protest. "The Council has already sent your father Atsego, to Assawickales near the forks of the Ohio where the gray Quaker has, with their permission, established a trading post. Atsego is to wait there until he receives a message."

Swinging his arm to designate two of the warriors, he went on, "These two will run with you, Tomawki, and guide you. As they run, they will tell you about events up to this time.

"We three," he continued as he pointed to the remaining two Senecas, "will see the woman safely to Atsego and beyond, if necessary. It is likely that Atsego and the Quaker, Kohl, will take her home from there. Now you must tell the girl and be on your way. The Shamans wait impatiently. Worry not. I will see her safely to any place she wishes to go, or die protecting her!"

"The Shamans are impatient," muttered Tom. "They don't even know if I survived the canoe trip from duTroit across the lake."

Ahnemose merely said, "Yes they do. The prophecy of Deganawidah is not complete. Atotarho and Dahweenet told us of more to come when the fighting is over."

Having said that, Ahnemose led the warriors out of earshot to give Tomawki an opportunity to explain to his woman.

Tom turned and knelt beside Nancy. Reaching out with both hands he cupped her chin and said softly, as he gazed into her blue eyes, "I have a destiny that I must fulfill, and, for now, I must part with you. My friend Ahnemose will see that you reach your home and parents. When I have finished my work, I will come to you, my love."

With that he kissed her gently on the lips and rose to his feet.

"Remember this. I will find you wherever you are!"

"I will be waiting for you," she answered. "I will be there."

Chapter XXXVII

The steady "pat pat" of moccasins as they jogged along the trail lulled Tom into a dreamlike state. A vision of Nancy kept running across his mind in a recurring pattern. It was the picture of her face looking after him as he turned for a last glimpse of her before he plunged into the forest. His reverie was brought to a shocking stop when a loud "whoop", seemingly in his ear, brought him and his companions to a startled halt. There was another whoop and "Hai, Tomawki!" as a Seneca outpost continued to shout and the cry was taken up from post to post along the trail. As they continued on their way, warriors came to greet them and a cacophony of sound followed them along the path. At last they reached an open clearing that served as the main camp. There stood the three sachems, Tehwanears, Sonosowah, and Dahweenet.

The Sachems were obviously happy to see him but greeted Tom casually, as if he had been gone for only a day or two.

"How is it that you are so casual?" he asked. "For all you know I could have been drowned in the lake, or I could be lying dead anywhere in this land where you could not find me. If you are seeking me as the Battle Leader, I can tell you that unless we are attacked, we cannot, in my opinion, extend ourselves further without endangering the fires of the Longhouse itself."

The two War Leaders merely nodded and waved their arms in the direction of Dahweenet. Smiling with obvious pleasure, Dahweenet laid his hand on Tom's arm and began to speak. "Atotarho never completed the Prophecy of Deganawidah until the Winter Council after you were first missing. As you know, Atotarho told how the prophecy said that the man would be a healer, and that he would also be a warrior who would lead the League to victory in battle. Indeed, that has been true."

Looking up at Tom, he continued, "The circle is incomplete. The work for the man who is named for his weapon is not finished. The two ends of the circle must be joined. In his continuation of the prophecy, Atotarho said that this warrior would add greatly to the strength and numbers of the Hodenosaunee. Finally,the Prophesied One would finish the prophecy by establishing a great peace throughout the land."

Looking steadily into Tom's eyes, Dahweenet continued Atotarho's words, "The Prophesied One will then disappear forever to that place from which he has come."

Speaking briskly, Dahweenet went on, "The eight belts of white wampum that your father, Atsego, brought to the Council at Kanatakowa are not a coincidence. They are Orenda!"

Deadly serious now, he squeezed Tom's arm and said, "There can never be a great and lasting peace for the Tuscarora shirt wearers, nor for the Hodenosaunee, until the hatchet is buried between our League and the mighty, Mengwe-speaking Cherokee Confederacy. Therefore, go you now to the banks of the Tennessee waters. Bring yet closer together the circle ends of the prophecy. Speak with the Cherokee."

Surprised, Tom looked over at the war leaders and found them nodding in agreement with Dahweenet, who spoke further, "Here are ten belts of white wampum to take with you. One is for the Cherokee, and one is for the English Governor in the Carolinas. The other eight belts of white wampum are to be returned to Nachininga. Tell Nachininga in the presence of all of his people that not even one belt is needed between brothers, let alone eight. Be sure that the English also hear you and carry with you a red hatchet in case the English should be inclined to argue. I am sure that you can explain things to them. Meantime our warriors will move south and east near to the Carolinas. Runners will accompany you close to the Tennessee and they will wait an hour away. Half will bring word to us of your success or failure with the Cherokee. The other half will then go with you to Carolina, should you require messengers there."

Tom, frowning with the burden of his thoughts, finally asked, "How do you think I should approach the Cherokee?"

There was a pause for a moment until Tewahnears broke the silence saying, "I know not how to approach them except that the approach must be bold yet with no hint of haughtiness or supplication, neither threat nor fear. You, Tomawki, will think of an approach and I know it will be right. The Cherokee already know of you and will respect you as a great warrior. In a manner of your own devising, let them know you are there, and they will come to you."

Dahweenet extended his hand and said to Tom, "Before you go, let me look deeply once more into your eyes. The words of the prophecy are such that, very probably, we may never meet again if, indeed, that is to be our Orenda."

Chapter XXXVIII

Nancy and Ahnemose had stood quietly and watched as Tom followed his two guides along the trail heading north until they disappeared over a hill and out of sight. When Tom's party could no longer be seen, Ahnemose beckoned to Nancy and the others and led the way eastward. Their trip was leisurely and without incident. Nancy smiled continually, reliving over and over again in her minds eye, their parting kiss and Tom's words, "When I finish, I will find you!"

Her three Indian guides, or guards, were so unusually solicitous in their care for her that she could only wonder who Tomawki was in the Indian world. Certainly, very few, if any, women were cared for by warriors, as was she. They helped her in climbing hills, carried her across streams, and stopped at any time they felt she might be tiring. Since Nancy had only a limited vocabulary, and that in Shawnee, and her guides had minimal knowledge of English, communication between them became a matter of smiles, and a few hand signals, but they got along.

Ahnemose was in no hurry. There was little of importance for him to do in the near future, now that he had found Tomawki and sent him on his way to meet with the Shamans. He was to rendezvous with Tomawki at the salt meadows a day's trot from the Tennessee, before the next full moon.

It was a clear sunny day when they reached the river of beavers and crossed, Ahnemose up to his chest in the water carried Nancy on his shoulders. They proceeded downstream on the eastern bank for a short distance. The water was still dripping from their clothing when they came to a clearing. There in the clearing, to Nancy's surprise, stood a cabin beside a small stream in this wilderness. Two men standing beside the door, a white man and a broad shouldered Indian. Their surprise at seeing a white woman was evident from some distance.

As the travelers neared the cabin, Nancy's surprise changed to excitement. She recognized the white man! She dashed past Ahnemose, who had raised his hand in the universal sign of peace, and grasped the astonished Quaker by the arm.

"Mister Kohl, Mister Kohl," she cried, "You are Mister Kohl aren't you, the man with the Broad Street store?"

Overwhelmed, the Quaker put his arm around the girl protectively and said, "Miss Nancy, is it really you? How did you get here, of all places?"

Turning to Ahnemose, totally bewildered, he asked, "Where did you find her?"

Barely understanding Kohl's broken Mengwe words, Ahnemose replied, "Tomawki found her. She is Tomawki's woman. He ordered us to bring her to you and to his father."

The Quaker now turned to Atsego and stuttered, "He saved her life!"

It would be some time before the confusion started by those words would become clear. Jakob meant that her life had been saved in Philadelphia. The girl had understood only one word in the exchange, "Tomawki". The three Senecas all nodded their heads in agreement with Kohl. Tomawki had indeed saved her life at Chillicothe. At the same time Atsego had assumed the same.

Jakob, finally reverting to English, looked at Nancy and said, "Tomawki, I believe that he's the one who cut your throat."

Nancy was totally bewildered. She said, "No. It wasn't Tomawki. That was Opessah. At least I thought he was going to do it."

Kohl thought she was befuddled after her long journey, and so he said no more about it. Instead the Quaker invited all to come into the cabin and share in the noon meal.

Following their meal, Atsego told Ahnemose that he intended to return to Charlestown himself, and that he would assume the responsibility for the delivery of Nancy to her parents. Ahnemose was somewhat reluctant. But the Quaker said that he, too, should accompany them, so the two Seneca warriors said their goodbyes and headed north along the Allegheny to the rendezvous point where the Hodenosaunee warriors were assembled. Jakob Kohl and Atsego made ready for their trip to return the girl.

Chapter XXXIX

Tom followed the warrior's trail to the ford on the banks of the Tennessee River. There he established his camp in the middle of the trail in full view of the South bank. On the log against which he usually leaned or sat, he laid out the belt of white wampum. The red hatchet and black wampum he placed in the open and covered with a fur, although the red handle could be clearly seen peeping out from under the cover.

He gathered wood and built a huge fire there in the open that could be seen for miles. Thus concluding his preparations, he sat on the log and lit a pipe filled with Kinnikinnick.

This repeated sitting and rebuilding of the fire continued for two days without event, though he could sense that he was being watched. On the evening of the third day he was sitting, as usual, on the log staring into the fire when he heard a splashing made by someone wading across the ford. Tom did not move except to reach down and pick up a burning twig on the edge of the fire and light his pipe. He could feel the presence near him and the gaze that was centered on his face.

Finally a voice spoke, "It is true what they, who first saw you, said! You are he who is called the warrior of Deganawidah's prophecy. I am Yahahnegwa and you are Tomawki, the Hatchet of the Mengwe of the Five Nations in the north, with whom we, the Cherokee, have battled over the years. My warriors could have slain you many times over as you sat here, but knowing you had a purpose with your white wampum openly displayed, they sent for me and I am here."

Having said that, the chief stepped around the fire and seated himself on the log beside Tom.

Tom puffed on his pipe and then held the pipe out to Yahahnegwa saying, "In my own mind I know not whether I am worthy of the role of Deganawidah's Prophecy, but my brothers, the great war chiefs of the Hodenosaunee, have asked me to carry the white wampum and the pipe of peace to the Cherokee. Under the circumstances you might not believe me to be the prophesied "Hatchet."

Looking at the Cherokee chief, Tom could see he had traveled far and quickly, evidently by horse. His leggings were wet to the knees where he had waded across the ford, but they were also wet on the inside of his thighs with the sweat of his horse. The pungent smell of the horse hung in the air. There was nothing fancy in the dress of the chief. He wore a plain leather cap with a single feather, a plain sleeveless leather jacket, leggings, and moccasins. He was unarmed save for the knife in his belt. He could be mistaken for a simple warrior except for his confident manner, which plainly told that he was the Chief.

Yahahnegwa reached out and took the pipe from Tom's hand and flicked his wrist toward the fire. For a moment Tom thought he meant to throw the pipe in the fire, but the chief smiled and said, "You are here to ask about the Tuscarora, The Shirt Wearers?"

Tom looked startled! The satisfied countenance of the Chief indicated that he knew he had hit home. How did you know this was my purpose, Great Leader of the Cherokee?" Tom asked.

"Deganawidah," answered Yahahnegwa, "visited all of the Mengwe, not just the Irakwai. He prophesied to the Cherokee of the coming of one such as you. That you are that man of the prophecy, I have little doubt, for he said that you would also carry the pipe of peace from the Tuscarora to the Cherokee."

"However, before you leave," continued Yahahnegwa, "though I have little doubt in my own mind, but I must tell you that some of the Cherokee do not believe in the prophecy. Nor do they think you could be the chosen one. You must prove another part of the prophecy. That may convince them."

Pointing to a man now emerging from the gloom of the surrounding forest, he said, "Manahkeeah, our Medicine Shaman, would question you about my mother since the Prophesied One is said to be a healer as well as a warrior."

An Indian at Yahanegwa's hand motion stepped into the clearing and approached them. When Manakeeah squatted on his heels

Scalpel And Hatchet

across from him, Tom asked Yahahnegwa, "What is wrong with your mother?"

The Cherokee replied, "Her face is bluish for many moons, her ankles are the size of gourds and she finds great difficulty breathing."

Manakeeah added, "Her heart beats faster than a running deer and her whole body is swollen."

Tom shook his head in wonder and smiled at the other two saying, "Now I too must believe in the prophecy for my Orenda is here within only a few steps."

Rising from the log he walked some ten paces to the clearing edge. Bending over, he pulled up two plants and returned to the fire.

Handing the plants to Manakeeah, he said, "This plant in England is called Foxglove and it aids the failing heart. Give the woman eight of the leaves three times a day to chew and swallow. At the end of five days she should be passing much water. The beat of her heart should be much slower and stronger. The swelling should be going with the passing of water. When the beat of the heart is steady, she must eat five leaves a day from now on. You must find more of this Foxglove."

Manakeeah rose and looked at Yahahnegwa saying, "I know the plant."

The Chief gazed thoughtfully at Tom for a moment and then said, "We will do as you have suggested and we will return in seven days."

He handed the pipe back to Tom and said, "We shall see if there is to be more smoking pf the pipe of peace when I return."

For the next six days Tom patiently took long walks in the woods and along the river. By the seventh day he was pacing restlessly around the clearing. He had expected the Cherokees to return after nightfall, but the sun was still high in the sky when he heard loud splashing in the ford that signaled the arrival of a party. Tom sat on the log and lit his pipe as Yahahnegwa rode into the clearing and slipped gracefully off his horse. Raising his hand in the sign of greeting and peace, he strode over to Tom and seated himself. When Tom offered the pipe to him, Yahahnegwa accepted it, nodded his head, and took a deep draft from the pipe.

Blowing out the smoke he spoke, "It is as you said. The mother of Yahahnegwa has put two years of sickness behind her. I am satisfied. But some of my warriors still question whether you are the Prophesied One."

At a wave of the Chief's arm, some fifteen warriors came out of the forest.

Yahahnegwa continued, "I would have you throw the hatchet at a target of my choosing to prove your name and role to them."

The warriors stood silently while the Cherokee Chief handed a hatchet to Tom.

Tom hefted the hatchet and said, "It is lighter that I like, but it will do. Where is your target?"

Bending over, the Chief tore a rounded white fungus growth, a little smaller than a man's head, from a dead tree. Placing the "target" squarely upon his own head, the Chief leaned against a tree trunk and said quietly, "Fear not, Tomaki, because I do not! I know that you are the man of the prophecy and you will not miss! This must be dramatic for this story will be told quickly from fire to fire throughout the Cherokee Nation and far beyond. Now throw the hatchet!"

Rubbing the flat of the hatchet against the side of his head, Tom started to speak but realized the Chief was right. Like an actor on the stage, he nodded his head and turned and walked away from the Chief. Suddenly he spun around and threw the hatchet with same motion. The weapon seemed to hiss as it spun in the sunlight across the clearing. The blade split the fungus in half and buried itself in the tree trunk. The handle vibrated in front of the Chief's nose as the two halves of the fungus fell to the ground.

Silence. Then the only sound was the gasp from every one of the warriors. There was a low murmur of voices and the warriors disappeared into the forest as quickly and as silently as they had come. The smile on Yahahnegwa's face spread from ear to ear.

He looked long at Tom and said, "We have both gained great fame this day. The story will be told over and over again. The Cherokee warriors will stay in their villages and a lasting peace will stand between the Cherokee and the Irakwai. The old feuds between family groups will no doubt continue, but once across the Tennessee there will be no more pursuit of raiders. There will be no war between the Nations in the future."

Pausing, he said, "Other than the observers I shall send to the white man's council with the Tuscarora, none of the Cherokee warriors shall cross the Tennessee or Santee. You have my word on this. If the Shirt Wearers wish to leave, they may leave peacefully as far as the Cherokee are concerned."

Standing, he faced Tom and placed his right hand on his chest. With a slight bow, he said, "I am honored to have lived this moment. I would be pleased to see Tomawki again. Now you must go and fulfill your destiny."

Then Yahanegwa was gone.

Chapter XL

The night was black as Tom slipped through the gate. The thin sliver of moonlight that came down through the clouds cast a shadow of the familiar pump across the yard.

"How many times," he wondered under his breath, "have I bathed in that cold water while Atsego pumped for me?"

He could see in the dim light that the yard was in good order and the hedges were trimmed. Knowing that Doctor Woodward had made arrangements in his will for weekly cleaning, he was sure the house would be likewise clean and in good order. Tom trotted across the back yard and leaped onto the roof of the low shed, heading across the roof for his old room on the second floor, as he had done so many times in the past. He had just reached the window when a voice from the darkness brought him to a halt.

"Warrior," said the voice, "I have spent many nights here waiting for your arrival."

Tom was moving at the first sound of that familiar voice, and in a trice had his arms around his godfather, Atsego.

At long last, after they had nearly exhausted themselves pounding one another on the back in the joy of their reunion, Atsego led Tom through the back door. They continued into the Doctor's study, where Tom had last seen his two godfathers. Atsego lighted a lamp that dispelled the darkness. When the comfortable and well remembered study took shape, quiet sorrow filled Tom's heart for he could visualize, once again, Woodward leaning on the mantle and, in matter of fact fashion, discussing his own coming demise.

Atsego leaned forward from his seat on the stool at the foot of the Doctor's favorite chair and said, "You know my joy in seeing you once again, but we will have much time later to talk of ourselves. Our time is short and there is much that must be discussed before the meeting of with the Governor General. I had expected you to arrive a week earlier than this."

Tom replied, "The Cherokee peace agreement was not to be made overnight."

"Peace with the Cherokee!" said Atsego in wonder. Truly, I was amazed when I learned you had come back from England, and I was stunned when they called you the Prophesied One, the Hatchet, the Healer, and the maker of Peace. However, when I had time to reflect on it, I felt the logic of it, and now I know it to be true. No matter how eager I may be to hear your story, it must wait, for time is short.

"Tawde, first of all," he said, "forget any worries you may have had about your woman. She is safe and she is here in Charlestown with her parents. She is, my son, a rare woman and well worthy to be the wife of such a man as you!"

Waving his hand impatiently, he cut off the questions that were about to pour from Tom's lips.

"It is enough for the time being," he said, "that she is here and safe and, yes, her parents are here also. You, the Prophesied Hatchet and Peacemaker have things you must do on the morrow. You must close the circle. Once done, you will happily have all of your life for the woman."

"Now," he continued. "This is the situation."

"Nachininga has been designated by the Shamans of the Tuscarora to be their designated spokesman. He has told the Governor General, Lord Faversham, that the Tuscarora wish to leave the Carolinas."

"Did I understand you to say Lord Faversham? Is he a very tall man?" asked Tom.

"Yes," answered Atsego. "Do you know of him?"

"Better than that." replied Tom. "If it is the same Faversham, I may have saved his life. I can feel a very strong Orenda about me."

Atsego nodded gravely and continued. "Nachininga has told the Governor that his people are desperate. They cannot stay here because their children are being kidnapped and forced to work in the fields. Twice have they taken up the hatchet because of this and twice have been soundly defeated by soldiers who are brought in. Unfortunately, those who send the soldiers have no notion of the plight of the Tuscarora. Or if those people do know, they do not seem to care. The Shamans fear further kidnappings if a move is not done quickly. They also fear attacks by the Cherokee if they attempt a long drawn out move to the Ohio. They would have to move quickly as a unit, but that is virtually impossible since they have no place to go. Nachininga asked me to secretly carry eight belts of white wampum to Brother Onas, and..."

Atsego stopped talking when Tom reached into his pouch and produced the belts of wampum.

Frowning, Atsego said, "I thought the belts were accepted?"

"They were," Tom answered. "I show them to you to let you know that I am aware of that part."

"Oh," said Atsego, "well when the Hodenosaunee prepared to send all of those warriors into the Ohio country to search for you, Atotarho told me to go to the gray Quaker, to his trading post at Assawickales, and wait for instructions. This I did. We, the Quaker, Kohl, and I waited with some impatience for several weeks. He had to wonder if you were still alive after sailing alone out into the lake so many months ago.

Then, at last, the warrior Ahnemose arrived with the news that you had been found and he brought with him the woman whom he said belonged to you. Ahnemose said that he was to see her delivered safely to her father in Charlestown."

Atsego looked at Tom for a long moment and smiled. "I cannot tell you of my joy to learn that you were alive."

"Ahnemose said you would go to Charles Town sometime in the near future. I knew at once what I should do. When I told Ahnemose that Kohl and I would assume responsibility for the safe delivery of the woman, he merely nodded his assent and departed. Where he went or where he is now, I do not know."

Tom smiled and said, "He is with me now and waits near the meeting grounds where the talks take place and the Governor sits in judgment."

Ahnemose grunted and said, "In that case I will tell you what has happened so far. The new Governor must make a decision after he has heard the arguments of both sides as to the punishment for the Tuscaroras for starting the two wars. Many settlers, especially the planters, led by a man called Manson, are demanding the Tuscarora young must be indentured for five years or more to work the fields. The Tuscaroras argue that that very thing is the cause of the wars in the first place. Some of the townspeople agree with them and

John.G. McConahy

think they should be permitted to leave peaceably. If so, where, when, and how?"

Chapter XLI

Faversham wearily blotted the perspiration from his brow with a fine cambric handkerchief. As he tucked the handkerchief back into his sleeve, he brightened perceptibly when he realized the speaker had finally finished. Manson had spoken at great length, nearly an hour, in the fierce heat of a Carolina day that was little relieved by the shade of the huge oak under which they sat. He was relentless in his demands for severe punishment of the Tuscaroras and he intimated that the settlers might well take things into their own hands if the Crown, that is to say Faversham, as the King's representative, did not take action.

Seven years of indentured servitude for the teenage Indians was the favorite suggestion for punishment. Faversham hated slavery in any form but even though he had a sneaking sympathy for the plight of the Indians, he could not see a feasible way of permitting them to leave as they had requested. If they were told they could leave, there was no question in his Lordship's mind that Manson and his friends would be merciless in their attacks and now the Tuscaroras were without weapons.

Delaying for more time to think, Favorsham watched Manson as he returned to his seat. In the meantime, the interpreters were giving the gist of the speech to the Tuscaroras. Faversham gestured to Nachininga. Speaking through the interpreter at his side, he told the Chief that he might reply.

As Nachininga started to rise, a figure on the edge of the Tuscarora group, a man who, had despite the heat been completely covered with a blanket, rose to his feet and threw off his cover. Ahnemose, clad only in leather leggings and moccasins stepped forward. A single feather dangled from his scalp lock and his face was streaked with war paint.

Stepping into the center of the clear area, he cast a threatening look first at Manson and then he spoke to Faversham.

"The speaker for the Tuscarora comes now," and dramatically he slowly raised his arm and pointed toward the town.

As all eyes turned toward the road leading to Charles Town, Ahnemose leaned over Nachininga and said softly, "It is well for you to sit quietly and wait for that one to speak for you."

Nachininga eyed the other carefully and whispered, "I do not know you, warrior, but looking at your scalp lock and paint, I think I know from whence you have come."

Again Ahnemose leaned down over the chief and spoke in his ear, "Hodenosaunee."

Nachininga looked hard into the eyes of the painted face for a moment and then he smiled and sat back down on the ground. Gazing around at the concerned and questioning looks of the other Shamans, he calmly said, "Our speaker comes."

The bewildered Shamans watched while he turned his own curious glance down the road.

Like Nachininga, Faversham too was looking down the road toward the town. A short distance from the assemblage, he could see a tall commanding figure striding toward him between lines of Indians who had suddenly materialized as though from the dust itself. All of these Indians were gazing in awe at the rapidly moving man. Everyone easily heard the Indians' "Hai's" of praise and approval.

Faversham's rather confused concentration on the approaching figure was broken when his interpreter laid his hand on the Lord's arm and said in a voice loud enough to be heard by all in the immediate vicinity, "Be very careful, My Lord!"

"The Indian who just spoke," he said waving a hand toward Ahnemose, who had turned away and was gazing like the others, down the road, "wears war paint. Moreover, he has not a distinguishing mark of any tribe that I know."

Dropping his voice a notch he went on further. "If you look about you, you will note that the Choctaw, Sioux and the other local tribes that have been watching the proceedings have quietly disappeared as though there were plague here!"

Unobtrusively, he pointed his finger toward the man entering the meeting area and added, "Many of those Indians seem to be regarding him almost as a god and are, unless I miss my guess, Cherokees, whom I never expected to see around here.

As Tom came walking up to the table, the interpreter said to Faversham, "This warrior as I know you have guessed, My Lord, is a white man. He wears war paint only on the right half of his face. Most interesting!"

Faversham leaned back in his chair and looked up at the strange and magnificent figure that towered above them. What Faversham saw was a rangy, well-muscled man, easily Faversham's own lanky height. The darkly tanned body was clad only in a breechclout and moccasins. In his left hand he carried a fairly large deerskin bag. A scalp lock of stiffened black hair stood straight up from his brow to the back of his head. The left half of the face was normal brown skin. The right half was covered with black paint with interrupted streaks of yellow and vermilion. The clear blue eyes that looked at Faversham were in striking contrast to the whole picture. There was a haunting familiarity to the picture for Faversham, despite the incongruity of it.

The Governor, about to speak himself, was visibly jolted when the newcomer said in the best of English, "My Lord, I am pleased to meet with you again, even in these strange circumstances. I am anxious to talk with you, but first, by your leave, I will now speak to the Tuscarora. They happen to be as confused as, I am sure, are you. I hope your interpreter," with a nod to the man, "will interpret my words for you."

Turning to the excited and nervous Tuscaroras, Tom raised his hand and said in a loud voice so all could hear, "I am Tomawki!"

A visible ripple of excitement ran across the Tuscaroras. Even as he noted in his mind's eye the attitude change in the Indians, Faversham rising, spoke excitedly, "Tom MacKaye, Doctor MacKaye, that's it!"

The interpreter gently pulled the Lord back into his seat.

"My Lord," he said, "that may be Doctor MacKaye to you, but look you at the faces of the Indians. To them that's 'Tomawki, the Hatchet'."

Looking at Tom with an expression of awe that nearly matched that of the Indians, the interpreter continued. "My Lord, that is a big medicine! I have heard of Tomawki, but I never dreamed I would ever see him!"

Looking for a moment at Tom as he stood before the Tuscaroras, he mused aloud to Faversham, "He is the Prophesied One, the

Battle Leader of the Five Nations. If he is here in war paint, you can bet there are Seneca and Mohawks, among others, who are nearby. And why are there Cherokee here? The Iroquois and Cherokee don't mix! Listen very carefully my Lord to my interpretation!"

Tom lowered his hand and reached into his deerskin bag. He pulled out eight belts of white wampum. Apprehension raced across the faces of the Tuscarora Shamans as they recognized the belts.

"The messenger, Atsego," he said, gesturing toward his godfather, who now stepped into the clearing so that all could see him, "carried your wampum to Brother Onas, as directed, but Brother Onas is across the great water, and his deputy would not see Atsego. In despair, Atsego let his Orenda lead him north from Philadelphia into a valley to which he felt drawn."

All were listening intently.

"In that valley," Tom continued, "he met a man, the same man that I had met in that same valley many, many moons before. This man was Shikellamy, a Pine Chief of the Hodenosaunee. When Shikellamy learned the nature of Atsego's mission, and then learned that Atsego was my father, he knew that this was indeed Orenda. He took Atsego to the Assembly of Shamans at Kanatakowa. When the Shamans heard Atsego's story, the council of the Five Nations refused to receive the white belts, and they have sent me to return them."

A muffled groan of despair ran through the Tuscaroras, as they perceived that their hopes were dashed. Tom turned to the table, reached into his bag and threw yet another belt of new white wampum on the table. Beside the wampum, he laid a red hatchet and then continued his speech to the Tuscaroras.

"The Shamans at Kanatakowa felt the Orenda also. So they sent an army of Senecas and Oneidas, headed by the war leaders, Sonosowah and Tewahnears, as well as the Peace Shaman, Dahweenet, into the Ohio country to find me so that I could be their messenger to you and to the white man in Carolina."

Faversham listened in excitement, but a tinge of fear had been introduced into the thoughts of the colonials as Tom continued to speak. At this point Tom's words were directed to both whites and Indians. I am here wearing two faces and two sets of moccasins."

When they all looked down, the group saw that, like the two sides of his face were different, so was he wearing two different moccasins. On the left foot was an ornamental beaded moccasin that might be worn on a festive occasion, while on the right foot there was a sturdy plain moccasin that could be worn for action.

With a deadly serious look on his face that none could mistake, he went on, "The Hodenosaunee, the Five Nations, have sent me here with this message. Return the eight belts of white wampum to Nachininga. Tell him that when brothers ask the Hodenosaunee for help, it is not necessary to send one belt of white wampum, let alone eight."

In the pause that followed, a sigh ran through the Tuscaroras and the interpreter seized the opportunity to whisper to Faversham.

"My Lord, this may be the escape for which you have been waiting. Look around you. All of the whites are suddenly aware of great danger, and well they should be! The word has gone around the people that this is the Battle Leader. He is not here to listen to meaningless word games!"

Breaking the silence, Tom spoke further. "Be at ease, my brothers. Lean back. As of this moment, you may rest knowing that you are protected by the shade of the Long House. We have made room for our brothers, the Tuscarora, in Hodenosauneega. We welcome our brothers. This is the message of the Council at Kanatakowa."

Nachininga leaned back and crossed his leg, his face wreathed in a contented smile.

Tom turned and addressed Faversham and the rest of the Colonials. Reaching down he picked up the belt of white wampum in his left hand and the red hatchet in his right. Raising his left hand with the wampum he said, "With this side, I represent good will and peace."

Turning so his left side was toward the white men, he continued, "As you can see, I wear no war paint. My moccasins are those of peaceful dress. In my hand I hold the belt of white wampum that Dahweenet, the Peace Shaman, has sent to you as evidence of our friendship. He hopes that the Governor will see fit to accept the wampum."

He then turned his right side to the Governor and added, "However, if the wampum is not accepted, Sonosowah and Tewahnears, the War Leaders, have sent the Red Hatchet to take its place."

Speaking now strictly to the settlers, he said, "This is deadly serious, if you have not already realized it. Yesterday the Seneca and Oneida crossed the James River. The Mohawk are even closer than that to this place. The Onandagas and Cayugas remain behind to guard the home fires of the Long House."

Reaching once more into his bag, Tom produced yet another red hatchet, which he laid on the table beside the first, and then pointed a finger at a warrior in full war paint who had just stepped into the open area. Touching the second hatchet, Tom said, "The great Shaman, Yahanegwa has sent that warrior with this token to tell you that the Cherokee...."

A loud gasp went up, and frightened looks flashed throughout the assemblage as Tom continued, "are already on the banks of the Santee and Peedee. They will cross if I give the signal."

Leaning against the table Tom said in a firm voice, "My friends, I can see the flames of burning homes from Massachusetts to Georgia. I can see that the English could be driven into the sea. The French would be left with the whole of the New World. You must let the Tuscarora depart in peace!"

Faversham stood and quieted the noisy talk that had arisen with a wave of his hand. He spoke in a loud, firm voice, even as he shook Tom's hand.

"The friendship of the Tuscarora and of the Five Nations is of great importance to us. The honesty of Tom MacKaye is well known to us. Let the move of the Tuscaroras begin without the hindrance of any man. We accept the white wampum from the Five Nations and will in turn send them indications of our pleasure in the peace. Tell the Tuscaroras their wishes are granted."

"That," he thought, "is a very nice solution to an otherwise impossible situation."

Suddenly Manson stood and cried out, "Ye damned turncoat renegade!"

Raising the pistol he had hidden by his side, he shot Tom full in the back at point blank range. The impact of the ball drove Tom to his knees where he grasped the table for support. With a desperate effort, he grabbed one of the hatchets from the table. As Manson turned to flee, Tom threw the hatchet with his last strength. Manson dropped to the ground. The red hatchet that split Manson's head was now stained a deeper red. As Tom's fingers slid across the table, he looked at Faversham's horrified face with agonized eyes and gasped, "tell Nanc... "

Without finishing, he slid to the ground.

Atsego dashed forward and cradled Tom's head in his lap. All of the others, Faversham, Ahnemose, Nachininga, and all who had been a part of the Prophecy knelt around him. Their tears mingled with his blood as it soaked into the dust.

The circle was now complete. The Prophesied One had "returned from whence he had come."

Epilogue

Radiant light poured through the window and fell on the face of the man in the bed. The rays seemed to burn his lids, so he steadfastly refused to open them. There was great contentment in the feel of the crisp, clean sheets that covered him, and in the comforting warmth that seemed to cling to his back. The warmth, he sensed, had been there for a long time and he murmured with pleasure. Finally he turned away from the burning light. He instantly regretted that move because a cool draft of air replaced the soothing warmth at his back. Blindly reaching out to try to find it again and draw it to him, he felt both warmth and silky softness. The startled cry of a female voice brought his eyes wide open, even as a wave of scented threads tickled his face. Looking up, he found a curtain of hair falling from around the beautiful face directly above him. Before he could speak, the door slammed open and a man burst into the room in answer to the cry.

The woman's voice, now soft and tender, said, "Atsego, go quickly and fetch my mother and father and a minister. He's awake at last. At least enough to make an honest woman out of me and give our unborn child a name."

Looking down at him, she smiled and said, "Oh, my dearest, I told them the warm body of a woman would bring you back to life a lot faster than a flock of hot stones at your feet."

Kissing him gently she raised her head again and called out, "And Atsego, tell all those Indian runners that have been cluttering up our yard these past weeks to go home. Tell them to carry word that 'The Hatchet' is no more. But you can also tell them that 'The Healer' is alive."

Then they got pleasantly warm again and Tom slept.

Author's note

In writing this novel, we have used actual historic events. We have also used the names of some individuals, such as Henry Woodward and Shikellamy, who were real people at the time. The history of the Mengwe is as accurate as we could make it.

All of the above being true, the reader is asked to remember that this is a novel! Doctor Thomas MacKaye and Tomawki are totally fiction and their actions are not true, nor are they historic! To our knowledge there was no such prophesied individual Battle Leader and Peace Maker, nor did any one man arrange for the acceptance of the Tuscaroras as the Sixth Nation of the Long House!

About The Author

John G.(Jack) McConahy was raised in Western Pennsylvania where his interest in early American Indians was nourished by the many Indian names and relics found in his area. As he became older he fished and hunted from the Hudson Bay in Canada to Florida's Key West. He became familiar with the Finger Lakes, Georgian Bay and the Hawk Mountain of Pennsylvania, where the famous warriors trail led natives of the Five Nations to join with the Tuscaroras in the Carolinas. It was this background which inspired " Scalpel and Hatchet", a fictitious story of a young prophetic leader who made this unity possible. McConahys earlier book," The Ronda Solution " was set in modern times in Ronda, Spain Doctor McConahy and his wife, Betty, together with their four children have tented across the nation from coast to coast, always enjoying the history of the country. Now that their children have gone, they live in New Wilmington, Pennsylvania and winter in Hobe Sound, Florida. Hobe Sound, we might add, is named for the Ho Be Indians.